Frosted Kisses

Rachel Roy

Published by Rachel Roy Independent Publishing, 2024.

FROSTED KISSES

First edition. September 11, 2024.

Copyright © 2024 Rachel Roy.

ISBN: 979-8987431467

Written by Rachel Roy.

Also by Rachel Roy

Journey Through The Gates
Through the Gate

Standalone
Growing Up As Fairies
How to Begin Homesteading: Start Small, Succeed, Expand!
Parallel Worlds
Last Kiss At Midnight
Frosted Kisses
The Ancient Ones

Watch for more at https://www.authorrachelroy.com.

Table of Contents

Frosted Kisses

Jessica is just out of a relationship and wants nothing to do with men for a while. A four day escape skiing with her best friend is the perfect getaway... until she learns Mellie's "little" brother, Griffin, will be there, too. Stuck in a tiny cabin in Vermont is ok until it's just the two of them alone in front of a crackling fire with no escape until the plows come through.

Chapter 1

He didn't have to be a jerk, but man was he good at it. She knew a breakup wouldn't be fun, but this. This was rougher than she was ready for.

"You're an asshole, Steven!" She flung the words over her shoulder as she slammed the door. To be fair, he might not have heard them through her throat clogged with tears, but he certainly heard her tone and understood her emotions. Well, maybe he didn't understand. He probably thought she was broken and heartbroken. She was heartbroken, but it was anger that sluiced the tears down her face. And she hated that she was crying.

He cracked a beer, flipped through the channels, and considered all the tasks he would have to do now that her cute ass had finally gotten sick of his shit. Sipping the Budweiser, he realized that she should have left a long time ago. He never really cared about what she wanted. He slugged back most of the beer and chose one of the Fast and Furious movies to watch. It didn't even matter which one. They all had fast cars and gorgeous women. Maybe he would call Grace. She kept saying she liked to cook.

HEART POUNDING, WHETHER from anger or the exercise, she wasn't sure. Jessica's best friend breathed hard beside her on that stair climber. "First," hard breathing, "who thought a stair climber was a warm up?!" *gulped air* "Second, you deserve so much more than him, honey."

"I know I deserve better than him, but it doesn't make this better!" Jessica was torn between relief at moving herself out of a stagnant and negative relationship and being completely heartbroken at losing the man she thought she would be with forever. "And we can switch to free weights if you want."

"No, we'll finish this damn 20 minutes. But I'm allowed to complain."

Jessica laughed, her first honest and full laugh of the day. Her best friend really hated the stair climber. They mixed up their aerobic warm-ups and Jessica loved the stair climber, so they did it at least twice a week, but Mellie did not enjoy it at all and usually had a steady stream of complaints.

Jessica's laughter turned to giggling hysterically, and she slid off the elliptical to a heap on the floor, half crying and half giggling. Mellie slid off her machine, wrapping Jessica in a hug.

"You know what? We need to distract you, get you to move on from that jerk!"

Jessica sniffled and rubbed her nose on the back of her hand. "I need a tissue." They stood up and walked over to the mirror. "Oh, my God, look at me!" Jessica pulled her long hair out of the ponytail and pulled it back up. Then wiped her eyes and blew her nose.

Mellie just waited at first and then said, "We're going to Vermont to hang out at the ski cabin in Burke. You are coming with us!"

"No, but I can't." Panicked, Jessica tried to come up with a reason she couldn't go, but her mind was annoyingly blank in this panicked state. Nervously, she redid her ponytail again.

"Yes, you can," soothed Mellie. "It will be perfect. We're just going for a couple days to make sure it's all set up for mom and dad to go up. We already have ski equipment there. I'm sure we can fit you. Or we'll rent at the mountain. We'll cook our meals right at the cabin, so it will cost you nothing. You just have to call in sick to work - a mental health day, and come up!"

Jessica was shaking her head, but Mellie just laughed, "Nope, it's settled. You're coming. Now let's go to the weight room so I can get this damn workout over with. Take out your frustrations with an extra five pounds on your bicep curls." Mellie grinned. Jessica hated that particular exercise as much as she hated the stair climber. This was why they were perfect gym partners.

"You're so mean to me!" But Jessica was laughing a little as she said it as Mellie dragged her over to the weight room. They took up their normal spot with two benches near the rack, with their two dumbbells each, and a kettle ball each. It wasn't crowded, so they didn't feel bad having the kettle ball and the dumbbells so they could switch between exercises in a tabata style workout.

Mellie let Jessica think as they switched through exercises and rests. She knew her friend initially said no, but then might change her mind. She wouldn't tell her that her brother was coming too. Her brother and his best friend. She would need someone with her to balance out all that testosterone!

Laying on her back, arms extended out, thumbs to the sky and gripping the dumbbells, she brought the bells to her ears. She hated this exercise, too. She was afraid she would misjudge and slam her face with a dumbbell. Her trainer had just laughed at her. "Yeah, don't do that." Expert advice, thanks, Ben.

The smell of sweat, and soap, and someone's really strong deodorant washed over her. Jessica tried to not think about the dumbbell potentially crashing into her temple. Mellie's phone chimed, and Jessica groaned in relief, not so much for the 30 second rest but for not concussing herself. "Ok" she said.

It took Mellie a moment to process that Jessica had said something. "Ok? Ok what?" Then her face lit up, "Ok, you'll come?! Perfect!"

The phone chimed again, and they repeated another 60 seconds of their previous exercise. At the next chime, they moved off the benches and stood by the kettlebells for the rest. As they started their 60 seconds of swinging the kettlebell through their widespread legs with one hand and then switching to the other, Mellie asked, "So yes? You will come with me? Yay!"

"I'll for at least some of the time. What days are you going?"

"You can come for the whole time. It's just four days. We leave Thursday and we'll be back on Sunday evening." Mellie laughed at her friend, "I know you have sick days available since you never call in. Call in sick on Thursday and Friday. You now have an appointment in Burke, Vermont."

Jessica stood in front of her door, chewing her lip. What was she doing? She hadn't been to Mellie's family's cabin in years, not since they were little kids. In fact, last time, one of the most vivid memories she had was Mellie's brother sneaking into the bathroom and throwing a snowball over the shower curtain onto her. She had shrieked like a banshee when that icy snow had hit her bare back. Nevermind that the hot water had melted it almost immediately. He had played some other prank on them, too. She couldn't remember what now. Mellie's mom had pulled her aside and tried to explain it was just because he had a crush on her. It didn't help.

She pulled out her phone to text Mellie backing out, just as it chimed: Here!

They were already here. She couldn't back out now.

Taking a deep breath, she grabbed her bag of clothes, slung her laptop bag over her shoulder and yanked open the door. Standing there with his hand up about to knock was Griffin.

"Oh, hey!" Jessica was startled by Griffin's proximity, but then his presence caused a sinking feeling in the pit of her stomach. "Why are you here?"

"Well, I thought," he gave his always happy, golden retriever grin, "you might want help to carry your stuff. Here, hand me a bag." He held out a hand to grab a bag.

"Noooo, actually I'm not coming. I was just about to text Mellie."

"Uhhuh, that's why you have your packed bag on your back. C'mon." He brooked no argument and slid her bag out of her grasp.

"No, but-"

He turned and walked towards the street, "C'mon."

Jessica huffed to herself and pulled the door shut behind her, checking the lock. That's all she needed, her ex to come over and barge through her stuff. The day after she broke up with him, she changed her locks. Not that a lock would stop anyone determined to get in, but it might be enough to make him rethink his actions. She huffed and grumbled under her breath all the way to the car.

The drive to northern Vermont was not too bad. The girls in the backseat, Griffin and his buddy in the front seat. The thing about driving north to Vermont was that the highway started at four lanes and dropped down to two lanes and often went from bumper to bumper traffic to almost no other cars at all. A little before they hit St Johnsbury, Griffin asked Mellie, "Pizza?"

"House of Pizza? Yeah! I'll call it in."

"Call it in?" asked Jessica.

"Yeah, I'll call the order in and we'll pick it up as we drive through Lyndon. House of Pizza is the best!"

"Uh, ok."

They stopped first to pick up some drinks and snacks. Then pulled in front of a brick building with the typical restaurant neon lights. "Cmon!" chirped Mellie as she got ready to hop out. "This is the world's best pizza!"

The overwhelming smell of pizza immediately filled the car as they climbed back in.

"Good thing we only have to go about 10 more minutes. That smells frickin awesome!" groaned Jason.

"10 more minutes, I'm dying!" groaned Jessica too.

Mellie put a finger to her lip and opened the top box silently. They each grabbed a slice, giggling. About half way through her slice, Jessica accidentally made eye contact with Griffin in the rearview mirror.

"Hey! No fair!" laughed Griffin. "Gimme one, too."

"Hey!" laugh-shouted Jason, too.

One pizza was almost completely devoured by the time they hit the driveway of the cabin.

"Whew, they did plow."

"I mean, I knew they were supposed to, but that would have sucked if we had to shovel now," said Griffin.

Unloading the car was done in quick order, but their breath clouded in front of them.

"Apparently, the furnace is not running, though." murmured Mellie "Yeah, that's all you. I got dinner."

Jason actually bled the lines after Griffin found some extra fuel out in the shed. The furnace quickly restarted then. The guys headed back to town to get more fuel. The ladies put away their food supplies and then brought the bags up to bedrooms.

"Which room do you want?" Mellie asked Jessica.

"Oh, I don't care," answered Jessica. "Any of them are fine."

"This is one of the biggest rooms. Here, you take this one."

"Ok, but I really don't care."

The cabin quickly warmed up. Plans were made to call for a full oil delivery the next morning and so the four of them settled in for an evening of wine, snacks, and cards. The end of a round of Cards Against Humanity at midnight had Jason complaining that his 4:30 wake up that morning had been a lonnnnnng time ago.

"I'll pick this up, y'all go to bed," offered Griffin. "You already brought my bags up, right?"

"Yeah, thanks!"

Jessica sat on the edge of the bed in her oversized t-shirt, stretching her neck from side to side. After finger combing her long hair, she picked up her brush and began pulling it through her still-tangled tresses. Finished, she put the brush down on the dresser, flicked off the light switch, and then slipped under the cover. The smooth bedsheets were still cold, but she knew she would warm them up quickly. She rolled over to face the window, staring out at the cloudless sky through the window, bunching the blanket up under her chin. Quickly warming up, she let the blanket flop away from her bare arm and threw a leg out. Emotionally exhausted, she fell asleep immediately.

Jessica started awake at the quick intake of breath when Griffin opened the door to his old room and saw a gorgeous woman laying on his pillow. This couldn't be intentional. All day she had acted like he was still the irritating younger brother to just deal with and humor. Seeing her bags in the room, he backed out and quietly closed the door.

Not really awake, Jessica rolled over and looked at the door, but it was solidly closed, just like she had left it. She fell back asleep immediately.

Glancing down the hall, Griffin saw one bedroom with the door still opened. Sure enough, his bags were just inside the door. He slipped in and sat down on the bed. He scrubbed his hand through his hair and rubbed his face. Damn, his sister's best friend had grown up, which he knew but hadn't thought about, and she was fucking gorgeous. What had Mellie said, that Jess had just dumped a loser of a boyfriend? She was rebound material, for sure. A little ski bunny four night stand and he wouldn't see her again for another 10 years. He could tap that.

Chapter 2

The day dawned bright and clear, with one of those majestic blue sky days reflecting off the bright snow. Mellie called around and arranged an oil delivery while Jessica cleaned up their breakfast dishes. Griffin pulled out ski equipment: boots, poles, skis, and bags to hold it all for everyone. Jason lugged in several armloads of firewood and stacked them by the back up woodstove.

"I do love wood heat," gushed Mellie, admiring Jason's strong shoulders. "It just has a different feel."

"Yeah, the dry heat is completely different than a furnace can do."

"Mom and Dad are thinking of switching this out for a pellet stove," Mellie continued. "I can see why. They aren't as strong as you, so it would be easier on them." She rubbed her fingers over his biceps and he grinned up at her from where he knelt, brushing up the bark mess he had made.

Jessica pretended she couldn't see or hear the flirting. All relationships sickened her a little right now. She was not going to be in any other relationship for a long time. Maybe a cat, yeah, a cat could be her new receiver of love. Or maybe a goldfish, even less of a commitment. She was rolling her eyes and aggressively scrubbing the frying pan from the eggs when Griffin walked back in. He took one look at her and then over to the two flirts. He laughed out loud.

"Save it for the slopes, you two. No need to lay it on so thick."

Mellie flipped him off and Jason snickered. "Yeah, right."

"Are we almost ready to leave?" asked Griffin.

"Damn, what's the hurry, bro?" asked Mellie.

"First tracks, y'know."

"Yeah no, we're not ready yet. I still need a shower."

"What? Why shower now? You're gonna be sweating through all the turns and be sore tonight?"

"Whatever." Mellie flipped him off again and headed upstairs to the shared shower.

"Hmph." Griffin rolled his eyes. Then turned to his best friend, "Maybe you should see if she needs help scrubbing her back." He flopped on the couch then and picked up a random book lying beside it. "Apparently," he grumbled, "we're gonna be here a while."

Still uncomfortable with the flirting, Jessica decided to make a soup to stay busy. She pulled out the crock pot and poured in some stock and seasonings while turning it to high. She peeled, then chopped some potatoes and carrots, then rough chopped some celery. Onion was peeled and chopped next, then a can of chopped tomatoes with Italian seasoning was added next. Jessica raided through the cabinets and freezer to see what else she could add. Once she poured in some corn and set rice on the counter to add later, she then turned the setting to low. It could simmer all day while they were gone.

Then Jessica moved to the living room, too. She pointedly put in her earbuds to avoid conversation and opened her laptop. Griffin watched her performance and rolled his eyes. He purposely sprawled out further on the couch since she had chosen the hard leather chair over by the window on the far opposite side of the room. It had to have a terrible glare on her screen, but whatever, she had always been snobby and unfriendly. No wonder he had tried to loosen her up with so many practical jokes.

He smiled then, remembering how he had slipped a cute little garter snake into her bag when she had slept over with Mellie one night. That one had been even better than planned. She didn't find it while at her house where he couldn't see her reaction, but had used the same bag at school and screamed loud enough in her history class that he had heard it in the science lab down the hall. He had recognized the scream and surmised what happened, but it wasn't until that afternoon that

Mellie confirmed it for him when she was telling their mom during the car ride home.

He chuckled again before turning the page.

"This is the type of place where we all work two jobs or have two houses. Which are you?"

"I guess I'm the one who works two jobs back home and has a friend with the two houses."

"Hey now, that works!" he laughs.

Griffin stood at the end of the bar. Jessica had her back to him, and he couldn't help but hear the flirtation. He also couldn't help the rise of jealousy.

"What can I get you?" the bartender interrupted Griffin's thoughts.

"Hey yeah, sorry. I'd like three drinks. Umm, what's on tap?"

The bartender smiled and rattled off the taps, then got Griff's order. As he got ready to carry them over to the tall table by the window, he said, "And whatever she's drinking," he nodded towards Jessica, "she's with us. I got her drinks, too."

The bartender just raised an eyebrow. "Ok, hers, too."

Griffin carefully carried the three icy glasses over to the table and then sat with his back to the window. His eyes were locked on Jessica, who was oblivious to him.

Mellie gave him a look and then followed his gaze. "Uhuh. Most people come here to look out the window at the view. You do not bother her. She needs to blow off some steam. She needs a one-night stand and you are not getting in her way."

"Yeah."

"Don't yeah me. I mean it. Leave her alone."

"Uhhuh. Do you see me over there?" But Griffin raised his hands in mock surrender and turned towards the window. "But really, a one-night stand?"

"Yeah, something simple and not long term. She just dumped loser's ass. Now she needs something easy and uncomplicated."

Griff glanced at her and nodded. Then looking back out the window, he quipped, "Oh my, look at the glistening snow marred by neon parkas haphazardly balanced on flimsy sticks and boards bouncing over what used to be smooth corduroy snow."

"Uhhuh, drink your beer, Grumpy, then we'll go back out. You can ask her if she's coming, then if you're so concerned."

Jessica's laugh rang out cheerily and Griffin groaned, grabbing his beer.

Jessica finished her drink and caught the bartender's eye. "Another?" the woman asked.

"One more," said Jessica, "I only have a $20 with me."

"No worries, I got these," said the guy at the bar.

"Oh, you're fine, honey, your friends over there have you covered." The bartender nodded to the table over by the windows.

"Oh." Jessica looked over and smiled at her friends. "In that case, I'll have another and maybe one more, but that's still my stopping point."

"Got it." The bartender poured her out another cider and slid it over.

"Your tip," smiled Jessica as she slid her $20 across the bar in exchange.

"You sure?" asked the bartender.

"Yeah, I was spending that anyway here and on you."

"That's ridiculous," scoffed the guy. Why would you tip her $20? You only had like $12 in drinks. A dollar a drink, baby. That's what you tip."

"No, that's apparently what you tip." Jessica spun out of her stool and grabbed her coat, goggles, and gloves. With her free hand, she picked up her glass. "Thanks for entertaining me on my break. Have a great day, Mike."

"Mark. But hey, what's the rush?"

"Sorry, Mike. I didn't realize my friends had come in." Jessica winked at the bartender and headed to the table by the window.

"Room for one more?" asked Jessica as she dropped her winter gear onto their pile on the ledge in front of the window.

"Of course," answered Mellie. "How's your arm? That was quite a tumble when you hooked that powder."

"Nah, it's fine. Might be a little sore tomorrow. But I thought it was a good time to rest. I haven't skied in years. Bars though, that I do know."

"So you're good to hit trails again?" asked Jason.

"Sure, for a little while. But you guys don't have to quit when I do. I tossed my laptop in the car before we left. I can do one of my freelance articles while I wait."

"Nah, we shouldn't overdo it, any of us. We'll ski a couple more hours, then head back, figure out some food, and hang out."

The snow was fantastic, so the three regular skiers stayed out until the lifts closed. Jessica quit an hour early, feeling the strain of muscles unused to the activity. SHe brought her gear down to the car and pulled out her laptop. Sipping a coffee, she scrolled through the waiting articles and chose one that seemed pretty mellow. She plugged in her ear buds and set to work. She glanced out the window now and then, sometimes catching a glimpse of her friends.

Seeing the chairs being folded up on the lift, Jessica powered down her laptop and gathered her stuff. She met Mellie and Jason on the stairs down to the lot.

"Griffin went down to the car to bring it up so we don't have to lug all our stuff down," said Jason.

"Makes sense," answered Jessica. "Where's his, I'll grab it."

"Cool, it'll take him a moment since he needs to switch boots."

The three of them carried the equipment down and leaned it on the rack by the bottom of the stairs.

Jessica checked her messages on her phone while they waited when suddenly snow splashed across her chest and face.

Mellie's laughter rang out, and Jessica looked up in time to see Mellie lob another snowball at Jason.

"You brat!" laughed Jessica, scooping up a handful of snow from the bank where it was still clean. Jason held her eye, and they both threw snowballs at Mellie. She ducked, and the snow hit the windshield of their car as Griffin pulled up.

Icy fingers and laughter filled the car as they headed back to the cabin.

Walking in the door, Griffin inhaled deeply. The smell of the ready soup was amazing.

"Oh my god, that smells like Mam's soup!" exclaimed Griffin. "I love that soup!"

Chapter 3 - Day 2

"T he closest Enterprise is frickin Littleton!" Mellie was not impressed.

"How far away is that? I don't know anything around here," griped Jessica.

"It's only like 45 minutes away," soothed Griffin. "We'll all drive over, get the car, and have lunch at the 99. Then, you'll drive to Boston and Jessica and I'll come back here to finish up the stove at the cottage."

"No, but, well, I guess that would work." Mellie could shift gears as quickly as anyone.

"Let me bring in some more wood so we can load it before we go." Griffin carried in three armloads of wood from the shed and dumped them in the iron rack by the stove. Jessica couldn't help but notice that carrying in the wood didn't seem to tire him at all. In fact, it brought out the definition of his upper arms. *What the hell?* That was not what she needed now! She did not need to imagine how strong those arms were, or how easily he could probably pick her up or wrap her up...

"That should be enough until tomorrow when the guy can come look at the furnace."

"It really sucks that me who wants to be here has to leave, and you two are stuck here feeding the fire." complained Mellie. "I hate my job sometimes."

"Eh, it is what it is."

Jason and Mellie took the back seat as they confirmed where they could drop the rental car off once they got back to civilization.

Enterprise was just a couple minutes off I93. Pick up was a little rough when they didn't actually have a car ready despite the confirmation. But there was a promise that there would be one ready in about an hour.

"It's ok, we'll go grab some lunch," ever the pacifier Griff herded them back towards the 99 Restaurant.

They agreed to sit at the bar. Mary, the loud bar tender, greeted them exuberantly and Pauline offered them menus and popcorn.

"An Angry for me, ok?" Jessica ordered before she hit the restroom. "Sure thing!"

The cool thing about chain restaurants is that their menu is the same all over. They could quickly order apps and choose their entrees without hesitation. Watching the game, listening to the restaurant wives harass each other behind the bar, and an hour and a half passed quickly.

"Well now, Jessica, what do we do with our time here? No real point in heading back to the cabin yet."

"Hmm, let's see what's around besides Walmart and McDonalds. Lol"

They both searched on their phones and found the world's longest candy counter at a place called Chutter's and a cool sounding hippy/wiccan shop called Aylakai and the Broom Closet.

"Sure, let's check it out."

Chutters was overwhelmingly crowded and after walking around exploring it a bit, they both left without buying anything at all. "That definitely would have been the best place as a kid," said Griffin.

"Oh, that would have been a blast. Sooooo many choices," agreed Jessica.

Walking around together was fun. There was no pressure to be anything except themselves, no one to try to impress or mince words with. It was just walking about a small town and popping in and out of stores. Finally, they were down to just grocery stores and libraries and they agreed to head back "home" to the cabin.

"Besides, it's getting kinda cold and windy. It feels like snow, don't you think?" asked Jessica.

"It is awfully dark," agreed Griffin. "We'll head back and feed the woodstove, then come up with a plan for dinner, maybe."

"Yeah, and not to be a spoilsport, but I do have some more work to do, too."

"Hey, that's great. I do too, actually." chuckled Griffin. "We can open a bottle of wine and sit in the living room. The Wi-Fi signal is usually pretty good in there, not so great in the bedrooms."

"Yeah, and the woodstove is cozy. Prefect, it's a da-" Jessica stopped short, but Griffin caught what she was going to say.

"A work date. Sure is."

And the awkward moment passed quickly thanks to his quick thinking. An hour later, Jessica uncorked and poured them each a glass of wine. Griffin had found two extension cords so they could each lounge comfortably with their laptops, and they were set.

"What are you working on?" asked Jessica.

"Eh, some cost analysis for my drop ships. Nothing very exciting. You?"

"Umm, well. I was invited to join a group writing about underwater ghosts."

"Underwater ghosts?"

"Yeah. So I thought of setting it in Atlantis and then I decided to make it like the location of Hunger Games. I think I'll keep it Young Adult, but I'm not sure yet."

"Oh, that could work. A challenge set within the crumbling city and ghosts there cheering them on?"

"Or maybe the ghosts don't like being invaded every year for the games...I'm not sure yet."

"When do you have to have it done?"

"Not until next fall, so I have plenty of time. I have another story that needs to be done sooner, and several other projects, but it's usually the freelance stuff that helps pay the rent and that's not nearly as fun."

"Yeah, I could see that."

"You used to read all the time. I guess that it makes sense that you like to write now."

"Yeah," she bit her lip in thought. "I think the best writers are also starving readers. Good writing lends to bettering our own writing. Y'know?"

"Hmm."

They worked then for a couple hours in companionable silence. It was actually an enjoyable day between two people who used to constantly irritate each other.

Griffin stood up to get a second bottle of wine. "Wow, look at that snow! It is really coming down."

"Oh shit. Do you think we'll lose power?"

"I dunno, but maybe we should figure out dinner sooner than later. We'll stay warm with the stove, but power out means no well water and no cooking."

"Right."

Looking from the kitchen, Griffin did a double take. He had a clear view into the living room and couldn't help but watch Jessica bent over, loading a few more pieces of wood into the stove. Those black TikTok leggings left nothing to his imagination. Well, nothing except how he could run his hands up those thighs, circle her waist, and pull her in against him. His hands could easily hold right onto a round ass like that.

Nope, time to end this fantasy. Actually Griffin began smirking just thinking about the fact that he had installed a little prank on her laptop - nCage. As soon as she looked something up, she would find that all her result images would be of Nicholas Cage. Harmless, but funny. He used to play pranks on her and Mellie's other friends all the time. Priceless. As he began pulling out pots and pans to cook dinner, it was his turn. He contemplated what other pranks he could play. It wasn't like she wouldn't know it was him, but he was bored. Oh, that singing lightbulb would be perfect if he could find it!

"Listen to that wind," commented Jessica as she stood back up.

"Crazy, yeah."

Just then, the lights flickered a little, but didn't go out. "I better hurry up and finish this cooking, though. That power doesn't seem too secure."

"Uhhuh," Jessica came over to the counter and sat at a bar stool to watch Griffin while he worked. "Whatchya making us? It smells good."

"Nothing glamorous," he laughed. "I found some frozen french fries, and we bought that ground beef, so burgers it is."

"I like burgers." Jessica smiled. It really was one of her favorite meals - yummy, kinda healthy, and depending on the toppings, it could be made a whole variety of ways. "Need any help?"

"Wanna slice toppings? We seem to have onion, lettuce and tomato."

"Sure, slide me a knife."

They worked in easy silence for a while. Actually, it was the most relaxed that Jessica had been in days. It wasn't that hanging out with Mellie hadn't been fun. Skiing had been fun, too. But this was calm, soothing in a way that she hadn't even realized she was missing.

"How do you like yours cooked?"

"Hmm?"

"Your burger? How do you want it cooked?"

"Oh. Medium is fine. I don't like blood dripping out of it, but I don't want it dry.."

Just as he was about to say, 'Almost ready, get your plate set.' the power gave a pop, a flicker, and then went out.

"Shit."

"Yeah. This is almost done though. So the residual heat in the pan might be enough. Any idea where the hurricane lamp is?"

"Is that the kerosene lamp?"

"Yeah."

"I think I saw it over there on the hutch. I'll look." Jessica used her phone as a flashlight and quickly located the lamp. A few more minutes produced the lighter that was *supposed* to be next to the woodstove.

"Aww, that's a nice light." Griffin was right. The little lamp did cast a nice warm glow over the counter as he served up their food. In another situation, it would have been romantic.

"Guess we won't be doing the dishes. There's no water."

They ate in companionable silence and then brought their glasses, a fresh bottle of wine, and the lantern to the living room.

"So tell me why he was such an asshat."

Griffin's question caught Jessica by surprise. She had been looking at how his hair caught the lantern light and shone with about nine different colors. "What?"

"You've always been loyal, so he must have been an asshat to screw it up with you."

"I mean, yeah." She grimaced. "He was. And I didn't want to admit that for too long."

"Yeah?" He had a question in his tone, but he didn't push her.

"He just wanted everything to be about him. My wants, my dreams didn't matter."

"Yes, they do. Your dreams matter." Griffin spoke softly, but he gazed. "What are your dreams?"

"No, don't matter."

"I think they matter."

Chapter 4

They kept drinking through the evening, sharing laughs and sharing dreams. Jessica soon loosened up and probably said more than she meant to.

The woodstove kept them warm enough, but eventually then ended up on the couch together, Jessica's legs across Griffin's lap. They lounged like old friends, but Griffin couldn't help but stare a little more. His sister's best friend wasn't gorgeous like a model, but she was captivating. She was intelligent, she was empathetic, and her sense of humor was fantastic once she loosened up.

The wine had loosened her up. Her walls had come down, and her laughter was genuine. Right now she was laying back, her head tossed back over a pillow against the couch arm, and her eyes were closed. Her face was flushed more than normal, and she had a happy little smile.

"You're watching me. I can feel it."

"Yeah, I am." Griffin smiled as he said it. Busted.

"Don't laugh at me. I know I'm buzzed." She wiggled down a little, getting more comfortable. Now her ass was right against his thigh and her neckline has slipped wider and lower.

Any other woman and he would be macking on her, but this was Mellie's best friend and the archenemy of his youth. She was also more than buzzed, and he would not take advantage of any woman who wasn't in complete control of herself.

"So, where would you live if you could live anywhere in the world without a housing bill?"

"Hmmmm, anywhere?"

"Uhhuh."

"Definitely near the ocean. I love the water!"

"Me too, girl." In fact, he lived about a half mile from the warm waters. Close enough to walk, but not so bad in the Atlantic storms. "Actually, I live close to the beach. You should have Mellie bring you down. Spend a week. I'm not a terrible host." He quirked a smile that she didn't see.

"Hmm, a beach vacation. I would love that. The sun, the water, the waves."

Griffin could just picture her laying out on the sand, a striped beach blanket below her, a cooler with drinks beside her, a book on her other side, and just laying there soaking up the sun.

"Yeah?" He tried to keep his tone light. "What would be the best part? What would you want out of an ocean vacation?"

"Hmm, feeling the sun just soaking in while I relax. I don't really remember the last time I could just relax."

"You can relax now."

"Yeah, I guess I can. Hard to work with the power out. I would only get an hour or so on the battery life." She made a face, and he chuckled.

"You need a new laptop if you only have an hour or so of battery life."

"Yeah, I need a lot of things." She was brutally honest for a minute, but then her shields came back up. "But at the beach all day. I would need snacks and cold drinks. Something to lay on. A book or three-"

"Three?" he laughed. But then he remembered what a voracious reader she had been, even bringing books to slumber parties with his sister.

"Depends on the books." She laughed too, then opened her eyes to look at him. "That's it. I'm simple. Books, food, sun, water, drinks, and maybe a sweatshirt if it's windy. Oh, and sunglasses."

"Right, need to cut out the glare of the sun on the page."

"Exactly." she grinned.

The window popped just then, making them both flinch, then laugh.

"It didn't even crack," said Griff. "Look, the light reflects off of it, but there's no disformation."

"Disformation?" asked Jessica.

"Whatever, pick on me for my words. But look, it's not damaged at all."

"No, but dang, that was loud!"

"Agreed, it was."

They chatted randomly into the evening until Griffin put her to bed without turning on the singing lightbulb - that would be a morning surprise when she could fully...appreciate it. He tucked her in and then left a glass of water by her bed. Luckily, there had been enough water in the pipes for two glasses of water. He was going to wake up thirsty as a race horse, too.

The next morning dawned sunny and brisk. The wind had died down through the night after blowing away the storm clouds. Sunlight now sparkled off every surface, whether ice, frost, or snow covered.

Jessica felt the sun shining brightly through her window and rolled away before opening her eyes. Normally she loved the sunshine, but her eyes already felt grainy and she hadn't even opened them yet. How much wine had she drank? She didn't even remember climbing into bed. Hopefully, Griffin had put wood on the stove before bed, because she was pretty sure she hadn't.

Groaning, she cracked her eyelids open and winced and she rolled her shoulders and neck. She slid out from under the comforters and padded to the bathroom. She flicked the light switch to see if the power was back on. A raucous song greeted her at a blaring volume.

"What the fuck?!"

She could hear Griffin's laughter from down the hall.

"Fuck you, too, Griffin!" A moment later, after uncovering her ears, she yelled out, "How do I make it stop??!"

"Just shut the light off."

"Damnit," Jessica muttered as she shut the light off and peed in the relative dark of the bathroom. A little light came in under the door and she could see well enough. Certainly well enough that she was not listening to that anymore.

After freshening up, she pulled her hair back, threw on a sweatshirt, and joined Griffin in the kitchen. He slid a mug of coffee over. "Peace offering?" he suggested.

"Hmmm." Jessica held the warm mug against her mouth as she savored the first sip in her mouth. She took a deep breath and mentally restarted her day. Peering over the rim of the mug, she said, "Morning."

"Good morning, Sunshine."

"I didn't hear it, but has the plow come through?"

"I didn't hear it either, but I haven't gone to look." He chuckled, "I slept pretty soundly last night."

"Yeah, me too. How much wine did we drink?"

"Well, there was one before dinner, but there are five bottles in the trash."

"Five?" she laughed out loud and then cringed. "I think I only remember two after dinner. No, maybe three. Definitely not four. That must be yours."

"Ah, no Little Lady, we did that together." Then more seriously he said, "We talked and drank pretty late, do you remember?"

Jessica did distinctly remember laying back on the couch with her legs thrown over his lap. But she did remember that he had actually listened to what she had to say and they built on each other. There weren't any insults or belittling comments. "I remember some of it."

"Yeah, it gets a little fuzzy at the end, but I do remember telling you to follow your dreams. I also know," he made a hushing wave as she went to interrupt. "I also remember that I absolutely meant that. You deserve to go after your dreams, don't ever let anyone stop you from trying. Planning together maybe, but don't let anyone kill your dreams."

"Hmm."

"I mean it."

"I know."

"Are you going to do it?"

After a pause Jessica said, "I'll try."

"Ok." Griffin accepted that answer for now. He grabbed the coffee pot then and offered her more.

Chapter 5 - Day Three - Saturday

Griffin and Jessica went outside together to shovel snow and check for wind damage. The heavy ice that had been such a problem was now covered with a few inches of snow. The shoveling in front of the doors and even most of the driveway wasn't bad. It was a workout, but it wasn't the heavy, wet snow that is exhausting to move. The only really difficult shoveling was next to the road where the town plow had pushed snow into the driveway. That snow which had melted a little and then refroze into a solid wall - that was difficult shoveling.

"It's today that the furnace people are supposed to come by, right?" confirmed Jessica.

"Yeah, that's what Mellie said."

"Good, I would hate to dig this all out for no urgent reason."

"Right," laughed Griffin with her. "No, it's important, not just back breaking."

They were both dragging a little by the end of the task, but Jessica couldn't help but notice how Griffin stayed in a good mood and kept her laughing while they worked. And he looked good doing it. Griffin couldn't help but notice that he and Jessica just kept chatting effortlessly. Once she warmed up, she had removed her jacket. Her long-sleeved blue shirt hugged her curves perfectly. She wasn't supermodel shaped, but he could just imagine how she could press up against him and feel just right.

"Whew, job done," laughed Jessica as she threw the last shovelful.

"I think it's time for a snack!"

"And more coffee," she agreed.

"And more coffee."

Stomping their boots off, they crowded into the mudroom together and bumped arms. It was like electrical shocks when their fingers touched and their eyes snapped together. They both froze for a moment, staring at each other.

I should kiss her. Griffin imagined just leaning forward and brushing a kiss against her red lips. But as he lingered, looking at her pink cheeks and windblown hair, Jessica shivered and then stepped around him. She brushed against him as she walked into the kitchen, but she kept her eyes down so he couldn't see her bite her lip.

Damnit. Griffin stood there for a moment, breathing deeply. When he followed her inside, Jessica had set a package of Oreos on the counter and started a new pot of coffee. Griffin slid onto a stool opposite Jessica and tore open the cookie package.

"So now what?" mused Griffin out loud. "We've met our responsibilities, now we just wait on the furnace guys."

"Hmm, yeah." Jessica leapt onto this normal conversation, willing her heart into a steady rhythm and not focusing on his gorgeous, sparkling eyes. "Too bad that we can't head out and ski or something."

"Skiing would be fun, but a no-go. So what now?"

"I mean, I have plenty of work to do, but that's not much interesting for you."

"I don't want to stop you from working."

"No, but I can write some later." She rolled her neck as it was starting to stiffen up. "I hate board games, but we could see if there's anything interesting on the shelves over there."

Griffin raised an eyebrow at her as she rolled her neck and half listened to her suggestion. Something about the shelves. "Your neck hurt?"

"Kinda, not really. It's just tight, or my shoulders are. It's fine. I just don't do a lot of shoveling."

"Yeah, I prefer little plastic shovels and sand buckets." quipped Griffin with a grin and catching Jessica by surprise with a beach reference. He stood up and came around the corner behind her. "Let me try something."

"What no."

"Yeah, it's not a big deal. Just let me rub your neck a minute." As he argued, he deftly began rubbing her neck, then rubbing and squeezing her neck and shoulders.

It felt so good that Jessica had to hold back a groan of pleasure. She did sag forward to lean against the counter and let her head drop forward. "Oh. That does feel good, actually."

"Uhhuh." After a few minutes, Griffin adjusted his stance, moving more to her side, wrapping one arm around her chest, above her gorgeous breasts, and then applying more force with his other hand against her neck.

Initially, Jessica tightened up at this change and his arm more intimately around her, but Griffin kept it impersonal and damn, it felt good.

After about ten minutes of neck and shoulder rubbing, Jessica felt a little guilty. "Turn about should be fair play. Do you have any sore muscles?"

Griffin huffed a laugh. "No, just neglected ones."

Jessica blushed as she could imagine quite a few of his muscles that she would like to be more acquainted with and would not neglect. "Ok then, how about I make us dinner later, pasta from scratch?"

"Yeah, pasta sounds great, and it is your turn to cook."

"Ok then." Laughing, Jessica spun out of his clutches and into the living room.

Griffin immediately missed the warmth of her body against his. She had fit perfectly against him, like their bodies were meant to be melded. Griffin took a deep breath and followed her to the livingroom. "Whatchya looking at?"

"I don't know. There's so many things on this shelf, some of it really old, I just thought there might be something interesting. Here's one of those blacksmith puzzles, if you want to try it out."

"Oh, I know this one. I used to do it all the time. It's easy." A few twists, and sure enough, he had the puzzle pieces separated.

"Ok, fine," Jessica retorted. "Let's see what else there is. There's some old leather books here, maybe they're histories of the area or something."

"Yeah, that could be cool."

She pulled them off the shelf. "This one is *Geological Formations of the Burke Glacial Pass* - not so interesting. This is.... *The Darling Estates - History of the Butter in the Northeast Kingdom* - really?"

"I think a guy named Darling is the one who built the big yellow mansion. He made his fortune shipping dairy to Boston or something."

"Oh, that makes sense, I guess. Oh, this one looks like a journal or a diary, this one too. I wonder who's they are?"

"There's no name on the cover?"

"No, and the first page doesn't say like Dear Diary, let me introduce myself, it just starts out talking about the weather.... Huh, they just had an ice storm, too. It says, 'Still stuck inside because of the roads being ice covered. I thought our guests could have left by now. Instead, I still need to entertain. Ugh.'" Jessica laughed. "I don't know who's writing, but I feel their pain."

"Let me see." Griffin patted the space beside him on the couch.

"There's actually two of them," Jessica was talking as she was walking over to the couch. "But the handwriting is different. Here, see if there's something more interesting than a snowstorm in that one."

They were silent a moment as they both began reading.

"This one is talking about finishing up a sale of something. I can't read it, and looking forward to a trip off their farm." Griffin loved puzzles, and he decided that's what these journals would be - puzzles to the past. They both settled in to read.

The weather has been decent up until now - a very late fall with no snow that stuck. Then a week ago we got a storm of 17". It was unpleasant and while it has packed down some, I think we have it to stay now. Then yesterday it warmed up enough to almost rain, it was sleety, and then it froze. Everything is frozen now. The MacClouds were supposed to leave yesterday, but with the weather, they chose to stay an extra night. Now, with the ice making any travel inadvisable, they're staying longer! The only plus side is that they help us shovel and do chores. I didn't have to go outside at all yesterday. The downside is that he, the younger one, eats a ton. He makes me laugh, though.

Jessica looked up. "Oooh, I wonder if this writer has a little crush on the visitors who are stuck here."

"Oh, yeah?" asked Griffin. *So far mine is talking about the heads of cows he has raised and prices of beef is almost as much as that for dairy, but of course dairy replenishes itself. Pretty sure they're selling their herd, or at least a chunk of it. He and his father are traveling for the sale and then staying with friends of his parents.*

"Do you think they're from the same time? Mine has visitors and the parents are friends, but I don't know anything else about them yet except that they're staying longer than planned because of the storm."

"Hmm, that would be weird, wouldn't it? Why would both their journals be here?"

"Well, let's keep reading and find out!"

"Hey, what's that beside you?" suddenly asked Griffin, looking over at Jessica lounging near him on the couch.

"What?" Jessica lowered the journal she was reading and followed Griffin's gaze. "Oh, look, it's a letter. It must have been tucked in here."

"Is it the same handwriting as the journal?"

"Why would she have saved a letter that she wrote?" giggled Jessica.

"Oh, right. That doesn't make sense, does it?" Griffin chuckled too. "I'll be honest, this journal isn't very exciting yet, focussed on damn cows. But maybe it's going to be more interesting, because they just finished the sale and he's irritated, apparently, that his dad agreed to stay for a cup of tea. He just wants to get to the vacation part of their trip."

"Mine has been complaining about the guests, but I think she has a crush on the young man. And maybe he has one on her, I can't tell."

"Oooh, tension! Two young lovers in denial."

"So, what does the letter say?" asked Griffin, leaning closer to look. "Hey, that looks like this handwriting!" He held the journal he was holding closer to the letter, and the handwriting looked the same, even the color of the ink.

"Wow, so your guy was writing my girl, and she kept the letter in her journal?"

"Hmm," Griffin waggled his eyebrows. "Read it, I'm invested."

My dearest Marion,

I hope this letter finds you and your family well. Hopefully, there have been no more terrible storms, nor have you had to shovel like when last I saw you.

Our farm has been busy this spring and will continue to be through the summer, of course. Calving happens year round, but there always seems to be more in the spring. And they always seem to be born at night, or in the rain. I really shouldn't complain though because the money that my father is making from selling these dairy cows will pay my university tuition. It excites me that you think I will become a competent veterinarian. How you described me interacting with your dog brings a smile to my face every day. Or maybe it's just thinking about you that makes me smile.

"Oh, he's so sweet," said Jessica with a smile. "I need someone like this."

"Yes you do, Jessica," agreed Griffin sincerely. "You absolutely deserve someone who will dote on you."

Suddenly brought out of the sweetness and completely uncomfortable in her own skin, with Griffin staring at her, Jessica abruptly asked, "And what about you? Do you have someone to dote on and who dotes on you?"

Chuckling at her discomfort, Griffin replied, "No, not now. Anyone I ever dated, I gave my full attention to, but there's no one right now. Mellie seems to think I need someone."

"Someone to tame your wild ways?"

"Something like that." He laughed again, then more seriously, "Someone to come home to. Someone to talk about our days together. To vent, to celebrate, or just to...I don't know, connect with."

"Yeah." Jessica chewed her bottom lip as she pictured this. "Yeah, that's what I want, too. Someone who I stay home with and chat with or someone to go out and hang out with. Someone I just want to be with."

"Exactly."

They both sat back then, thinking about past relationships and hopes for the future. Neither wanted to settle into marriage yet, but something more serious than random dates was what they both craved. A serious relationship to add to their daily life.

"More wine? Or more coffee?" asked Griffin to change the mood. "Who knows how long we have to wait for these repair guys."

"Wine already?"

"Why not?"

"True. Umm, yeah, they both sound good. Surprise me."

Griffin grinned and moved into the kitchen. He began brewing coffee and chose a bottle of red wine. He found one of his grandmother's trays and placed on it the bottle, two glasses, plates, a box of wheat thins, a bowl of grapes and a plate of sliced cheese. Then, when the coffee had brewed enough for two cups, he poured out a mug for himself and a mug with just the amount of cream and sugar he had watched her add earlier.

He brought the mugs over and set them on the coffee table.

"Oh, perfect," said Jessica, picking up the mug and holding it against her cheek, absorbing the warmth.

"But wait, there's more!"

"More?"

"More." Griffin laughed as he brought over the very full tray.

Jessica laughed freely as she saw the full spread. "You, Griffin, might be the perfect man." He grinned and then she added, "Except for your damn pranks!"

Chapter 6

The day passed blissfully uneventfully, with Griffin and Jessica passing the journals and love letters back and forth. Luckily, the furnace repairman showed up before they had too much wine and gotten too silly. Unfortunately, the piece for the furnace would have to be ordered and might not arrive for a day or two.

"I'm sorry," Jessica was trying to stay calm on the phone with her supervisor. "I didn't intend to stay longer, but there have been unforeseen circumstances and I won't be back for Monday morning. I'm calling you now so that you can plan accordingly."

Griffin could hear the screeching on the other end of the phone and couldn't help but roll his eyes at the absurd reaction. Jessica wasn't even late yet as they still had another day originally planned here for the ski vacation of the four of them. Too bad that Mellie and Jason had had to leave so early, but he didn't actually mind the alone time with his sister's best friend.

Deciding to offer an assist, he caught her eye and grinned at Jessica. Then he clattered a fork into the sink, and banged together two small frying pans.

"No, I'm sorry, I couldn't hear what you said over this background noise," Jessica said into the phone. "See, they're working on it right now." More screeching was the reply.

Griffin came over and stood beside Jessica, "I'm sorry ma'am, there really is no fixing it as it stands now. We'll need a few days to get the right parts in."

"I'm sorry just a moment," Jessica said into the phone and then held it against her thigh, effectively muting it. "You're," she laughed with

Griffin, "incorrigible. But I really appreciate it. The old hen is really giving me shit."

"Yeah, I could hear that." He rubbed his ear as if in pain. "I didn't know human voices could actually reach that pitch."

Jessica schooled her face back to seriousness and took a deep breath. Then she returned to the phone conversation. "Look, I really have to go. But there's just no way that I'll be in on Monday. I'm sorry." She quickly ended the call as soon as she could, and Griffin helped by tapping a handful of spoons against the sink, creating an interesting rattle-tap.

"Well, that was fun." Jessica sighed. "Why do people have to be such jerks?"

"You realize that most people aren't, right?"

"The ones in my life mostly are."

Switching tactics, Griffin tried again. "Why do you work there?"

"Duh, bills and things. I kinda like to eat, y'know."

"No, I get working. But why do you work *there*?"

"Ohh. Well, 'cause they hired me. I get to focus mostly on writing up packages for them, so I get to write, which I generally enjoy. It's just the people who are jerks."

"What if you had a different job where you could mostly write? Or write an edit?"

"Yeah, there actually aren't that many of those jobs, not that pay decently, anyway."

"My company has an opening, I'm pretty sure."

"Your company?"

"Ok, not MY company, but the company I work for." He had to chuckle at her tone. "But I am a supervisor there and I can put in a good word with the supervisor of our copy department. I bet you can have the job. You might need to provide some samples, but I'm sure that won't be a problem."

"If you have an opening like that, I'm sure you also have about 200 candidates. I can never match up against them."

"First, you could certainly hold your own." Griffin was completely serious now. "Second, there aren't 200 candidates because we haven't advertised it yet. It was discussed at the board meeting the night before we came here. Third, you deserve to work somewhere that you are appreciated and valued. My company is very, very good at that." He could see the wheels turning in her head. "Plus, your position can be partially remote if you like. Come to someplace like this on a Sunday, work some of the time, ski midweek without the crowds, then return to the office on Thursday or so."

"Hmmm," was all Jessica said. But she was chewing on her lip again.

"Think about it," said Griffin lightly. "You don't have to decide right now." He paused, then added, "But it would make me happy."

She looked at him with her huge blue eyes. "Really?"

"Yeah, you're fun to be around. You're fun to work with."

"Thanks, you're not half bad yourself."

My dearest, Marion,...

There were about ten letters in the journal altogether. All written to dearest Marion. She had tucked them into the journal as she received them, but they were well worn, as if they had been read and reread repeatedly.

That night, Jessica lay in bed for a while, thinking about Marion and her sweetheart. It was too bad that the letters she must have sent in return hadn't been saved. She could see that they courted through his first year of veterinary college and then the journal was filled. If there were other journals and letters belonging to Marion, Jessica hadn't found them yet.

They were so sweet, both journals and the one-sided letters. To begin with, the two had just been shoved into sharing space as their families were friends. However, it seemed that quite quickly, they were smitten with each other as they were stuck together for hours because of an ice storm. Jessica couldn't help but see the parallel to her situation.

Last time she had spent any time with Griffin she must have been about 22 and it was Mellie's graduation, but that had been one afternoon and no more than ten minutes of conversation. Before that had been in high school, but they hadn't really been in the same crowds and he seemed to do everything he could to irritate both girls. The worst had been the summer of her freshman year, before he was even in high school. He had done everything he could to irritate her, from frogs in her backpack, to mud in her hair, to telling some random boy that she had a crush on him (she didn't even know the boy), to tying all her shoelaces together. ANYthing that would bug her, he seemed to do. As well as the constant jumping out to scare her from behind any door or corner. It was a wonder she hadn't had a heart attack that summer. He had matured though, once he got to high school, two years behind the girls. By then, their circles just didn't really overlap.

Now, he was sweet and observant. Now, he had outgrown the gangly arms and irritating body language. Now he was handsome, smart and funny. No, she wasn't falling for him! How cliche would that be, trapped in a snowstorm and falling in love? No, not just falling in love, but falling in love with her best friend's brother, whom she used to hate. How many tropes could her life be squeezed into?! Yet he was a nice guy now, and she was enjoying being stuck in the cabin with him. She would probably enjoy hanging out with him just about anywhere.

Her thoughts then rambled on to Griffin, offering her a job at his company. Could he even do that? But he had offered to call that supervisor that evening just to prove he wasn't pulling her leg and that it really was a viable possibility. She had nervously declined, so he promised that they would in the morning. It seemed like he really wanted her to take the job.

Then she would have to move and there were so many things to consider, but the one thing in her favor was that the lease on her apartment was up for renewal next month. She hadn't filled out the paperwork yet. She could just up and leave if she wanted to. Her job certainly had no hold on her except the convenience of stability. If she gave them two weeks' notice, they would have no reason not to provide her a decent recommendation. Except that the shrew might not just for spite. After all, she would have to do Jessica's work until they hired a replacement. But, the way Griffin spoke, it sounded like she wouldn't even need a recommendation beyond him. He seemed to think that her work samples would speak for themselves. She had a decent portfolio of freelance work. More of her own fiction writing, but also HR work, advertising assignments, a game that she had created and scripted, book reviews that she had written, and entire OSHA based safety manual and quiz that she had created,... maybe Griffin was right. Maybe she did have enough to show her skills in a variety of styles.

Maybe she should say yes.

Chapter 7 - Day 4 - Sunday

Griffin lay in bed, staring at the moonlight reflecting on his ceiling for a very long time. Mellie's best friend had grown up from a cute college girl to an amazing woman. He wanted very much for her to realize how amazing she was. Clearly, she had been hurt and certainly she didn't see her own worth. The last thing he should do now was fall for her and hurt her on a weekend fling.

But here was where his emotions sputtered. He didn't want a weekend fling. He could have easily had her when they were sharing those five bottles of wine. They had both been happy and loose and it would have been easy, and potentially messy, to bed her then. But he didn't. Sure, he tucked her into bed and then he couldn't help but stand there staring, imagining her naked and him laying beside her. But he had been a gentleman, if a drunken one, and went to his room alone. All day, reading the journals together and puzzling together over the romance of his grandparents. At least he assumed it was his grandparents. The whole time, he had wanted to reach out to her. He had wanted to cup her soft cheek with his hand and pull her in close for a kiss. He so badly wanted to taste those lips.

He groaned and rolled over. He was going to need a cold shower at this rate.

It was perfect though for her to come work at the same company as him. She could have the spare bedroom at his place until they found her an apartment. He had seen her writing, and he knew, even if she didn't believe it, that she was a perfect fit for the writing that they needed. Plus, he had seen her editing work. She could really improve their website. She deserved a job that would appreciate her. She deserved a team to work with her, not a group of people that she worked for.

Maybe she wouldn't like it, but he knew he really wanted her to take the job when Mike offered it to her. He had already texted him, and Mike said that they hadn't even posted the job yet, so if she was any good, she could have it. Griffin assured him that she was more than qualified. They would talk more in the morning, but Mike was drawing up a tentative offer to be adjusted after he and Jessica spoke.

Griffin smiled. At least that he could do for her. Now if he could just get her imagined naked body out of his head... As a teenager, she had an athletic body with toned arms and legs. She had the perfectly flat belly and huge tits even then. Now maybe she wasn't quite as svelte, neither was he. He laughed to himself. But he could imagine that her extra plumpness now would fit just perfectly against his extra plumpness, too. What he wouldn't give to feel her heavy breasts in his hands while he thoroughly kissed her.

A cold shower. He would definitely need a cold shower.

What if she was hesitant, though? What if she wouldn't take the job thinking she wasn't good enough or scared to move to a new town? Would Mellie help him? She must want the best for her best friend, right? Or would she just assume that he was scheming like he did so often for her college roommates and friends? He had used her for several hookups and had not been a gentleman. Of course, the girls hadn't expected anything more than one-night stands then, but still.

Because he did want more with Jessica. He wanted her to have this job because it would be good for her. But he wanted her to have this job so she would work with him. So she would be near him. Because he wanted to be her everything in a partner. So how should he convince her to trust him? How could he convince her to date him without it seeming like the job was just a side benefit he could offer her? She deserved the job, and it had nothing to do with him except that he knew about the opportunity. But would she believe that? And if she didn't, how could he choose between the noble and right thing versus this undeniable, insatiable want that he had. His happiness mattered too, didn't it?

Griffin came down the stairs and saw Jessica standing in front of the fridge. Hearing his steps, she looked over her shoulder at him.

"I was going to make you breakfast as a thank you for setting up this interview," Jessica started, "but we seem to be a little low on options."

"Now see," replied Griffin, "I intended to come down and make a good breakfast to boost your confidence in this interview that you're going to ace." They both laughed. "So let's go out."

"Out?" she repeated.

"Yeah, you know, out to eat. My treat."

"You don't have to buy me breakfast."

He could see her getting her hackles up. "Oh no worries," he grinned to diffuse her, "You're in charge of buying food for lunch."

Jessica grinned back, "Ok, deal. Where do we go?"

"Let me introduce you to the Miss Lyndonville Diner. Locals and tourists eat there. You can have breakfast, but they also serve lunch foods all day. You can't beat their home fries or their triple decker burger."

"Ok, let me put on going-out-in-public clothes."

"Yeah, I don't think anyone will care what you wear."

"But, I do."

"Fair point. I'll start the car so it can warm up."

"Ok, I'll just be a minute." Jessica ran up the stairs and, true to her word, came back down three minutes later wearing jeans, a hoodie, and her hair pulled back in a high ponytail. She slung on her winter coat and leaned over to tug on her boots. "So we just need to go to Lyndonville for both the diner and a grocery store?"

"Yeah, unless you want to go exploring. We're not tied here. We could go back to Littleton if you want."

"Nah, I don't need to go anywhere else." Then quickly she added, "It's not all about me though. We can go wherever you want."

"Lyndonville is fine. Besides, you probably want to add your little finishing touches to your portfolio to send to Mike."

"Mike. Michael Greenley, the supervisor you'll talk to after breakfast."

"Oh."

"Don't get yourself all nervous. He's a great guy and he'll love you and your work. I just know you're going to want your portfolio to be perfect and you're going to double-triple check it."

Jessica chuckled. "Yeah, I want to do that."

"Right. So we'll eat something that someone else cooks for us. Then we'll stop for some groceries and then come back for you to nerd out."

"Hey, pretty sure we're both a little nerdy."

"Hmm. Maybe."

Breakfast was crowded and happy. The diner was an obviously popular spot, but it was easy to see why, with friendly waitresses, quick service, and good food. Then, Whites Market for groceries. "Why exactly are there two Whites Markets, like a mile and a half apart in the same town? Like none of the buildings here are more than three stories and there's like 50 streets in town. They can't have that much shopping to do?"

They quickly found the ingredients that Jessica wanted except the special semola flour, but she decided she could make do. They even cheated and bought homemade pizza dough to make calzones for dinner.

Looking over at their basket, Griffin asked, "What exactly are you going to make for lunch?"

Grinning, Jessica answered, "Pasta."

"Pasta? But there isn't any."

"Cooking helps me think, sometimes. I guess it depends on my mood." Jessica chuckled and shrugged. "I thought I would make pasta today."

"Like from scratch?"

She nodded.

"And the sauce, too?"

Again, Jessica nodded and began putting items onto the belt.

"Girl, you just won my heart."

Jessica laughed like it was a joke, but a blush stained her cheeks. Griffin pretended not to notice and began bagging items into one of the very small paper bags available for $.04 each.

I'll make sure you always have time to think. If you're going to cook Italian food from scratch whenever you need to be pensive, I'll throw riddles and puzzles your way every day."

Jessica snorted, "I cook Indian from scratch, too."

"Curry?"

"Yup."

"I'm in love."

The cashier was obviously entertained by the two of them. "You better keep her happy, she's a keeper," she not-so-quietly whispered to Griffin.

"I'm trying," he agreed.

She looked cute, working behind the counter in the kitchen, a little smudge of flour on her cheek, and wisps of hair escaping her ponytail. The sauce she had simmering also smelled amazing.

"So where did you learn to cook?" Griffin asked Jessica as he sat on the opposite side of the counter watching her.

"My aunt taught me a lot of the nuances. I learned the basic steam, slice, broil from my mom, but it was my aunt who refined my skills. It depends on my mood though. Sometimes I enjoy cooking and sometimes I cook just to eat, y'know?"

"I don't love it, but I don't mind it," he replied. "But my idea of making spaghetti is boiling water, pouring in the pasta from the box and then browning ground beef and dumping in a jar of sauce. If I'm really feeling it, I might chop up veggies to add to the sauce." He laughed, "Mine smells nothing like yours."

Jessica just made a depreciating looking shrug. "Eh, we'll see."

"Hmmm," added Griffin. "And the only time that I have seen pasta made, like mix the ingredients, roll it out and make it, was in the mafia movies with the old country Italian wives."

"Well, I'm not Italian, so this probably won't measure up."

"Stop it."

"Stop what?" she looked up at him, clearly confused.

"Stop downplaying yourself. You clearly know what you're doing. Don't downplay it."

"Hmm."

"I mean it. And don't do that on the phone with Mike either. Be confident about what you do. You're damn good at it or I honestly wouldn't recommend you like this. I would have, well, I wouldn't have offered anything at all, but if you had asked, I would have just said I would look to see if there were open positions. I'm recommending you because I believe in you. The least you could do is ALSO believe in you."

"Hmmph."

"Uhhuh."

He let her stew in those thoughts for a few minutes. Then, to break the silence, "You know what else they had a lot of in those mafia movies?"

"Noooo, what?"

"Wine. I can handle that. Do you want red or white?"

"Umm,"

"Relax, I've seen how you can handle your alcohol, plus you're gonna eat. Red or white?"

"Red please."

"Done."

Griffin wasn't wrong. The wine did loosen her up and relax her a little, but she didn't get tipsy or sloppy. He was also right that Jessica's homemade pasta and sauce were some of the best food he had ever tasted. The flavors were complex, with all sorts of flavors bursting and dancing in his mouth, but nothing was overpowering or too much.

"Oh. My. God. Apparently, you should be a chef."

"Noo, there's just a couple of dishes that I make well. This is one of them."

"That soup the other night was amazing, too. Just like Gram's."

"Eh, a couple of dishes."

"Yeah, whatever." Griffin just laughed at her. "Obviously, we'll need to practice accepting compliments. Meanwhile, you cooked so I clean. Nahuh, no arguing, I insist."

So then it was Jessica's turn at the counter and Griffin washed the dishes and cleaned up. Their easy conversation and banter just flowed like they had been doing so for years, not days.

Storytelling seemed to be natural for both of them and soon they had shared stories of drunken escapades at bars, and stories of counter-irritating, annoying coworkers. Now they were on dream vacations.

"I love the idea of just living in a beach house, laying in the sun half the time, and sitting on a porch the rest of the time. The salty air swishing the curtains, but it's warm all the time." Jessica was describing her perfect setting. It was the same as they had talked about the other day.

"Uhhuh, sounds perfect. And it could rain at night, you know, to keep things alive, and you could fall asleep to the sound of the rain and then have the sun again the next day."

"Right!"

Maybe an occasional beach barbecue or party or something to mingle with people, but mostly just relaxing with a book, or writing."

"That's a book, too," offered Griffin with a smile.

"OK, smartass. Either relaxing reading or enjoying the calm while writing." Jessica laughed along with him. "I don't know if I could just do that, though."

"What do you mean?"

"I feel like I could do that for a week or so, but then I would feel lazy or guilty."

"Why?"

"I dunno. Good Catholic upbringing, I guess."

"You're Catholic?"

"No. I was raised Catholic."

"Oh, that makes more sense. But I meant, if you were writing a book, or reading to perfect your craft, why would that be lazy? Why feel guilty?"

"Perfecting my craft. I like that." Jessica chewed on her lip while she thought. "I guess it would be so nice that it wouldn't feel like work. At least in my idealized daydream."

"Hmm," Griffin was struggling to focus on her words, instead mesmerized by her beautiful lips nibbled on by her own teeth. He couldn't decide if he wanted those delicious lips against his, or if he wanted her teeth biting his own lip.

Chapter 8

Griffin pulled his attention away from Jessica's perfect lips to look her in the eye. "I haven't told you where I live yet, have I?"

"In Graniteville?" asked Jessica

"Well yeah, but details."

"Umm, no, I guess not. Oh yeah, you did mention not far from a beach, right?"

"Let me grab my phone, to show you pictures, hold on." Griffin realized this could be what wins the deal. It was the second time she had mentioned living in a beach bungalow. His place wasn't quite that, but almost.

Jessica watched Griffin run up the stairs two at a time, hand sliding up the railing as he went. She could imagine that same hand guiding her back as they walked along a beach. She really loved being by the water and could imagine the two of them playing in the water and laying in the sand. She was quite sure the sun would show off angles of his body that she would find quite tantalizing. Her best friend's little annoying brother was neither little nor annoying anymore. Those arms could wrap right around her and hold her securely while sitting on a sandy beach at night. She could imagine the warmth of his body against hers, safe and strong.

Jessica shook her head and had a swallow of wine. Definitely not a ladylike sip, but a swallow as if to swallow away the image.

Was he really off limits? Was there any reason other than she would never escape him and would have to see him at least every few years?

Griffin came jumping down the stairs again, two or three at a time. "Here, this is the beach near my house." He slid the phone to her and then sat on the stool beside her.

"Oh! That's gorgeous! This is outside your house?"

"Nope, but only a few minutes' walk from the house. So almost all the benefits, but none of the cost." They both laughed. Then Griffin reached over and slid to a different picture. "Here, keep swiping, these are pictures of my house. It has the beachy theme, even though it's not quite on the water. I love it."

They were pressed together shoulder to shoulder now, and somehow her arm was linked through his from his swiping to a different section of photos. Neither seemed in a hurry to disentangle.

"It's rustic and coastal combined. I love it!" Jessica easily gushed at the photos, truly loving the open, sunny design.

"Yeah, it's a two bedroom, a few minutes from the beach, and a big backyard with a swing on the porch. We could do a backyard barbeque if that'll work?"

"We can?" she giggled.

"Yeah, it'll be your housewarming party once you move in."

"I'm moving in?"

"You should. It only makes sense, since you'll be working with me. The commute is amazing, and you'll feel like you're on vacation when you're home."

"Hmm. I feel like we're kinda rushing here. We don't even know if I have the job yet."

"You'll have it." Griffin didn't even hesitate, assuring her. "But even if we didn't know, you should still come live with me. You need to do what makes you happy, and moving out of that shabby apartment should be right near the top of the list."

"It's not that bad!"

"Girl, I saw it when I grabbed your bags."

"It's not-"

"It is. It's not like falling down dangerous, but it's old, shabby, and probably cheap as fuck, but not pleasant to be in."

"It's not that bad."

"It's not that good."

"Hmm."

Griffin looked at his watch. "Ready to talk to Mike?"

"Oh, shit, really?"

"Relax, you'll be fine. He's easy to talk to."

"Uhhuh."

"He is. Just pretend you're talking to me. Not as cute, though."

As expected, Jessica giggled at that and was back at ease. She took a deep breath, "Ok, let's do this."

"Thatta girl."

Jessica reluctantly pulled back and unwrapped her arm from his, sliding his phone back to Griffin. The loss of warmth between their bodies was immediate.

"Want me to just call and get you two started, or do you want me to hang out?" asked Griffin.

Jessica looked at him with wide eyes and bit her lip.

That's so fucking adorable.

"It sounds really rude," she began, "but do you mind if I do most of it alone? I'm nervous enough and having you listen, too..."

"Hey, no worries, I get that." Griffin gave her a smile. "Nah, I know you'll do fine, but it's like driving along all perfectly legal and a cop comes up behind you. You can't help but feel a little nervous."

"Yeah, kinda like that. Irrational, but-"

"But still real. I get it. I'll call, introduce you, and then excuse myself."

Jessica fairly exploded out of her chair at the counter as soon as she logged off the zoom interview. She did a little squeal and spin. The interview had gone really, really well. Mike had asked general questions, but then had delved deeper into her creative style and formatting opinions. They had gone over a couple pieces that she had done as a freelancer, what the customer wanted, how she might have done it differently, what he would have asked for. After almost 45 minutes of chatting that felt much, much shorter, Mike said he would email her an offer today and gave her a rough quote that was about $1500 a month more than she was making now.

What Mike didn't tell her was that he was sure about that much money, but wanted to include the potential of bonuses and more than just the standard benefits package. He wanted to actually create a supervisory position for her. But he didn't want to raise her hopes unless he had it approved.

"Hey, Griffin!" called Jessica up the stairs.

He almost immediately bounded down. "It went well, didn't it?"

"I think it did."

"Oh, I know it did." He held up his phone to show her the text he had just gotten from Mike.

She's a rockstar! I'm going to Dave to see about upping the benefits package before I send her the offer.

"Wait, there're different levels of benefits? He didn't say anything about that."

"Yeah, there's," Griffin paused for a moment. He could read between the lines and saw that Mike was looking at a supervisory position, but if Jessica didn't know that he didn't want to blow it. "There are often tiers, depending on what level you work at."

"Hmm. I guess that makes sense." Then grinning again, "Let's go celebrate!"

"You're on! Give me a moment to change."

"Yeah, me too. I put this shirt on to interview, not to wear for the day."

A few minutes later, they were ready.

Griffin waggled his eyebrows at her. "You look awesome. Everyone is going to be jealous of me taking you out." In her form fitting soft blue sweater, dark blue jeans, and hair pulled back in a ponytail, Jessica looked completely comfortable and cute as hell.

"You look pretty good yourself there, stud." Jessica thought he looked awfully cute in his black pullover and jeans. Who else in this area wore cowboy boots in the middle of winter? "I don't know where to go," said Jessica as she pulled on her gray, faux fur-lined boots.

"Well, somewhere with booze to celebrate," said Griffin with a chuckle. "So not the diner. And this calls for more than pizza, so not the Lyndonville House of Pizza. Hmm. There's a restaurant in Island Pond that's really good. The hotel is built over the river, but I don't remember what it's called now. It's gone through so many name changes over the years. Good food though."

"I'm game. I don't care where we go."

"Cool."

"It's about 45 minutes, or maybe half an hour. It's a pretty drive up 114, too."

"Isn't that where all the moose hang out?"

"Yeah, in the summer at dusk you'll see a ton of them! It's sometimes not a fun ride in the wintertime, but the roads are fine today, I think."

"No worse than anywhere else, I bet."

"True that. It's worth thinking about up here since there are so many places without cell service, but it's the middle of the day. Let's go." As he was talking, Griffin had loaded up the woodstove as full as he could, which would hold it until fairly late that night if they decided to stay out really late.

Chapter 9

"Apparently, It's *The Essex Tavern*," giggled Jessica as they pulled in.

"Yeah, apparently."

Parking was a gravel parking lot beside the building. In front of them was an outdoor seating area by the river that looked like it might have a small stage set up. "That must be really cool in the summer," said Jessica.

"You know, for a little town here, Island Pond does a lot with live music."

"Really?"

"Yeah, through the summer they have live music over in that park across the street. Behind that gas station is a deck that has some sometimes. Here apparently."

"Hmm."

Together they walked to the front of the building and then further down to the actual entrance. Inside, they were greeted quickly and then led past a suit of armor and up the stairs into the tavern.

"What can I get you?" asked a perky waitress in a black t-shirt.

"Umm, what do you have for cider?" asked Jessica.

"On tap we have the Original Downeast or we have canned peach Downeast, we also have-"

"Nope, that's good. I'll take an original Downeast, please."

"Sure, and for you?" the waitress looked at Griffin.

"Sam Adams is on tap?"

"Yup, we have the Winter Lager on tap."

"Yeah, I'll try that."

"Do you want a sample or a full drink?"

"Oh, I didn't know you did samples." The waitress smiled and nodded, waiting. "No, that's fine, I'll do a full drink," said Griffin with a smile.

"Perfect," said the cheery waitress. "I'll grab your drinks and then be back to see if you're ready to order."

"Sure, thank you."

"No problem!"

The menu was complete with as many options as a large chain, but more unique. For example, there were cheese curds served with maple butter, and poutine with your choice of gravy. There were many entrees from pub burgers to grilled fish, steak tips to a turkey club.

The waitress was back quickly with their two on-tap drinks and shared the specials. They decided to order the cheese curds to start while they figured out what else to eat.

"Sure thing, honey." It really wasn't clear which of them that the waitress was calling honey and Jessica wondered if that was intentional.

The cheese curds were amazing and so was the soup and the chicken marsala and whatever that seafood special was. They ate it all, sharing each other's plates and laughing away. They were totally stuffed and happy.

"I cannot eat another bite!" laughed Jessica.

"No kidding," agreed Griffin, "but I want to keep having fun. I also want a nap."

"Oooh, a nap does sound good." Jess bit her lip in that adorable way. "Let's go back and take a nap and then find someplace playing music."

Griffin lifted his eyebrows and started nodding. That sounded almost perfect. Why hadn't he thought of that? "Are we napping alone or together?" he flirted.

"Well, I don't know." Jessica looked through her eyelashes. "If you're not a blanket hog, my bed is big enough, but not if you snore!"

"No snoring, got it."

Jessica blushed bright red. What am I doing? *I'm not really inviting him to my bed, but I just did! Oh, my god!*

Griffin grinned at her discomfort. "You know, if you spoon with clothes on, it doesn't count as spooning."

"Oh yeah, who made up that rule?"

They carefully stepped around the puddle of slush as they walked back to their vehicle. It was a great excuse for Jessica to avoid looking directly at Griffin, but she couldn't help but look sideways to watch his reaction.

"I did just now. You get the benefits of cuddling and not being alone, but there's no pressure for more."

"I'll hold you to it."

"And I'll hold you."

"You're quite the flirt, aren't you?"

"And you're not?"

"I have no idea how to flirt!"

"No Jessica, you are incredibly good at flirting."

They moved on then to talking about the songs on the radio.

Suddenly, a huge snowy owl swooped over the road ahead of them.

"Look at that. Owls are amazing," breathed Griffin, leaning over the steering wheel and watching the owl for as long as possible.

"I LOVE snowy owls!" exclaimed Jessica.

"For sure. They are one of the prettiest."

"Have you ever had one fly over you? Probably all owls, but you feel them, you don't hear them."

"Really? They're that quiet?"

"It's unreal!"

Soon enough, they were back at the cabin. The stove was still kicking out heat, so after shucking off their winter coats and boots, they both headed to the stairs. Griffin stood by Jessica's door and ushered her in. She walked past with her eyebrows high and head tilted in silent question.

"Ladies first," he grinned. "I don't know about you, but I think we should nap naked."

"Yeah, no," laughed Jessica. "You're not really coming in, are you?"

"Of course I am." He grinned at her, then waggled his eyebrows, "Unless you can't handle it."

"Noo, I can handle it."

"Ooh, what are you handling?"

"Oh, shut up! You're incorrigible."

"I am." Griffin pulled back the blankets and flopped on the bed. Then patting the space beside him, he said, "C'mon. We can sleep fully clothed. It won't be as comfortable as sleeping naked, but less awkward, maybe."

"Hmm." Slowly, Jessica laid down beside Griffin. He moved up against her, but left some space between their bodies and draped an arm over her waist. The heat between them was like a furnace. Surprisingly, Jessica relaxed and soon, they were both breathing deeply.

Jessica woke up first. Not surprisingly, she and Griffin had pulled closer together during their nap. Instead of his arm draped over her side to her belly, it was now draped more over her chest. Her back was pressed right against his chest and belly. She couldn't help but notice how she fit completely against him, like they were formed to fit together. It could easily be a sexual embrace, but she was awake, and he wasn't; she chose to just absorb the comfort of being held against a warm body in muscular arms.

"What do you want to do next?" Jessica jumped at the sleep-gravelly voice in her ear. "Sorry, didn't mean to startle you."

"No, I uh, I just didn't realize you were awake, too."

"Hmm," He wiggled a little against her, loosening his arm over her, but not moving away at all.

"I woke up a moment before you, I think. I heard your breathing change."

"That sounds kinda creepy," Jessica giggled, "But I know what you mean." She considered rolling over to face him while talking to him, but chose to stay right in this magical moment. "Live music right? Didn't we say we'd try to find some music somewhere?"

"Uhhuh. Probably more food, too." Griffin yawned contentedly. "But it's your day to celebrate. We do what you want to. You want to go get a mani-pedi? We'll do that."

Jessica snorted, "Yeah, that seems likely."

"I'm just saying we do what you want to do."

"You know, I've never had a manicure, let alone a pedicure?"

"No?"

"No. Not today either."

"Ok. They probably wouldn't want to touch my hairy toes, anyway. They may be relieved at your choice."

"They? They who?"

"I dunno, whoever would have been available."

"Uhhuh. You probably don't have hairy toes, either."

"Hmm."

"Let's just lay here a few more minutes, then we'll look up live music venues."

"Yup, sounds good." Griffin lay silently, breathing deep and evenly until Jessica thought he was asleep again. Again, his voice was in her ear. "I'm not, you know."

"Not what?"

"Not asleep. I felt you relax, but I thought I should tell you I'm still awake."

"Oh."

"Just content."

"Yeah," Jessica's brow furrowed at the thought, unsure, "me too. And I don't even know why this is so comfortable."

"Hmm. It just is."

When they disengaged from cuddling, Jessica picked up her laptop from beside the bed and scooted into a seated position. "OK, I'll look up local places, and you'll tell me how local it is and the vibe-"

"I don't know if I know the vibe."

"Since apparently anything within three hours is 'local'."

"Yup. Sounds right."

"Ok, so in Montpelier-"

"That's kinda a poke. Like an hour plus away."

"Hmm, ok. How about Newport?"

"Newport, Vermont, sure, make sure it's not Rhode Island. Actually, I guess that's an hour too, but it seems easier. It's a quick drive up or back. I guess it's the roads."

"Sure." Jessica had no idea what he meant, but she just went with it. "So there's music at Jasper's, Tavern on the Hill, and the Eastside"

"I haven't heard of Jasper's, but both the Eastside and the Tavern are nice. They both have good food. The tavern is basically a bar, the Eastside is a whole restaurant. The bar is in the main dining room, plus they have separate dining areas for events. It's way bigger."

"Ok." Jessica chewed against her kip as she kept scrolling. "So they're possibilities. Looks like the Littleton Freehouse and Taproom have music."

"No. Check their prices. They're very hoity-toity."

"Ok, let's see. Shit, $18 for a house salad?" She laughed. "Yeah, no. Where else...?"

"Newport is fine." Griffin scratched his chin. "Food, booze, and music."

"There's the Red Barn in Danville, too."

Danville is maybe a little closer, not a terrible drive, but it's small.

"Small isn't necessarily bad."

"No, the atmosphere is good, I hear, but the food isn't great."

"Hmm."

Jessica and Griffin broke apart to shower, dress, and get ready for their evening out. They called ahead and ordered grinders from Lyndonville House of Pizza. Jessica was surprised that Griffin ordered exactly the same thing she did - a whole wheat roast beef grinder with mushrooms, but no onion.

They chose a table in the corner and people watched while they ate their grinders, chips, and sipped their beer. There were families, there were singles, there was a table of late high school or early college kids, and everyone was just casual and relaxed. It was the perfect place to grab a bite to eat. Being able to see right into the kitchen also meant the owners could see right out. George and Lynelle made a point of saying hi to many friends as they worked.

Once they were done, and cleared their table, Griffin ordered some baklava, the honey sweetened pastry, to go. "We'll want this later."

"We will?"

"Oh definitely. It's amazing, in and of itself. But we both crave a sweet bite at night and that's all you need of this."

"Ok."

"Trust me."

"I have been."

"True. And see how well it's working?" Griffin raised his eyebrows while grinning, and Jessica couldn't help but laugh along. He was right though, it had been an amazing day because she had done the interview that he had suggested.

"I do trust you."

"Good." Griffin smiled sincerely at her. Then he grabbed her by the elbow. "Let's go. Danville is only like 15 minutes from here and the music starts soon."

Just as he had said, it was a short drive to The Red Barn. The parking lot was about two-thirds full and the lights inside spilling out the windows, with twinkle lights along the fence rail leading up, gave a festive and welcoming feel as they walked in.

No one met them at the door, although several people looked at them, or at least at the opened door. They quickly found a table for two or three off to the side near a window. After seating, they spun around to see the menu on the wall. As Griffin had guessed, there were not many food options. Jessica found herself distracted, looking into the brewery itself as well as the food prep area.

"What are you thinking?" Griffin broke into her thoughts.

"Hmm? Oh, I forgot to check the menu. I got distracted, I guess. It would be cool to watch them actually making their brews. It's cool that you can see right into their workspace, right where they pour their recipes into the tanks and test, and whatever they do."

"You're right, it is cool." Griffin paused, then grinned as if about to ask her to take a risk. "Wanna be daring and try one of the house brews?"

"I don't see a cider up there. So no, probably not. I don't actually like microbrews."

"What? Why are we at a brewery, then?"

Jessica laughed. "I don't like microbrews, almost ever, but I do like music."

"Ahh. I see." Griffin bobbed his head side to side, "Ok, I get that. I'll go see what else they carry on tap. I'm gonna try the Foggy-Whatever-It-Is and I'll find you a cider or a light-flavored IPA."

"Thank you."

Griffin was back at the table a few minutes later with two frothy glasses. His was considerably darker than Jessica's. "They had a cider. Tell me what you think." He watched her carefully and laughed when she scrunched up her face after the first sip. "Well, that's a no."

"No, not exactly. The initial apple taste is good, it's just very floral afterwards, like I just ate a daisy."

He could completely imagine her in a field with a daisy held between her lips. The image of the sun kissing her face, the wind teasing her hair, and the flower tickling her soft lips. He wanted to be there right now, not this crowded brewery in the middle of winter.

"Hmm, as pretty as you would look eating daisies, you can pick a different drink. They kept the card, so you can just add to the tab."

Jessica blushed bright red. "No, I'll finish this. We'll see what's next."

"Ok, what's the name of the band again?"

"It's a couple, something about 'wellness'..." Jessica chewed her lip, trying to remember what she had read.

An older woman at the table next to them leaned over, "They're called 'Alive and Well' super cool people. I think she could sing the menu and people would pay to listen."

"Yeah?" asked Jessica. "That good?"

"Oh, they both are." The woman nodded. "I've heard them several times. We both have." She nodded at the gentleman at her table and he smiled in greeting. "The way they play together makes them so good. You'll see."

Just then a tall man and a much shorter woman climbed up on stage, and did some fine tuning to their guitars. They murmured to each other and then they began to play. Griffin caught Jessica's eye, and she grinned back.

Chapter 10

The small brewery slaked their thirst, the music got their souls happy, and eventually Jessica and Griffin left The Red Barn Brewery happy and sated with life.

"This was a good night, thank you, Griffin," said Jessica as they walked to their car.

"Good. I'm glad."

They were quiet but comfortable for the half hour drive home. Snowflakes danced through the air as they drove, but it was pretty not stormy. Moonlight glistened off the snow-covered fields. Just as they were pulling up the road close to the cabin's driveway, a large white owl flew overhead.

"Was that an owl?" asked Jessica, not quite believing it.

"Sure was. I think it was a snowy owl."

"I think so too. It was pretty big."

"Yeah. They're super cool. I wonder what it's hunting?"

"I always think it's amazing how they can hear little creatures tunneling under the snow and snatch them right out. Not so great for the little mice, but cool for the predator."

Outside of the car, Jessica stretched her arms out wide and savored the bright moonlight. "Wanna go for a walk?" she turned quickly and surprised Griffin with the question.

"Um, sure." He wasn't about to say no to her for almost anything. There was a dusting of snow now which muffled their steps, and the bright moonlight reflecting off the snow gave them plenty of light to see by.

"This is always what I picture in the story 'Twas the Night Before Christmas.'"

"Hmm, and the moonlight gave the luster of midday below...?"

"Yeah." Jessica grinned. She had read that story about three hundred times while babysitting, plus listened to it endlessly through four years of band practice in high school for their winter concert, when some elementary kids narrated the story and the band played. SHe knew it almost perfectly word for word, but seldom found others who did.

"Me too." Griffin smiled down at her as he stood beside her at the end of the driveway. "Which way?"

"I don't think it matters."

"Hm, then this way," he turned left. "We usually drive the other direction."

"Sure."

Griffin reached out then and slipped his hand around hers. It was warm and strong, but Jessica was certain he would let go if she pulled back even a little. Which she had no desire to do.

They didn't speak at all until they reached the top of the little hill. The trees to their left opened up and they could look down and across a field to what seemed like a stream below. If it was a stream, it was frozen over because they couldn't hear any water. Suddenly they felt, more than heard, a swoosh overhead.

"Oh shit!" said Griffin, ducking a little.

"Wow," laughed Jessica.

They stood watching the path of the large white owl, nearly silent in its flight.

"I have no idea how to tell the males from females, do you?" asked Jessica.

"Nah. I just think it's gorgeous."

"Probably male then. Most female birds are drab."

"Maybe." Griffin was working out how to turn that into a compliment towards her, being unlike a bird, when suddenly the owl dove. "Look!" he breathed.

A moment later the owl rose up, huge wings shaking off the snow, and still silent.

"DId it get it?"

"I don't know, I can't see."

"Me neither, but I imagine so. Actually, I have no idea how accurate they are. I just assume they have better luck than not."

"The owl, you mean."

"Yeah."

Down lower in the field, movement caught their eyes. First, one deer hesitantly came out and then another followed behind. They both crept into the field, looking this way and that and then standing stone still.

"This is an amazing place to be," breathed Jessica.

"Better than a beach?" asked Griffin.

"Nope. I'll take sun and heat any day. But this is gorgeous and peaceful."

"You fit right in."

"What do you mean?"

Griffin tugged her to face him. I mean, it's gorgeous here, but so are you."

Jessica felt heat rush to her cheeks, which were already pink with the chill in the air.

"I,... uh..."

Griffin watched the snow catch on her lashes as she stumbled through the compliment. "We'll work on that," he murmured. With his free hand, he rubbed the back of his thumb against her cheek. "I want to shower you with compliments every day until you believe every one of them." Gently, he slipped his fingers under her chin and lifted, tipping her eyes back to meet his. "You are gorgeous, Jessica." He bit his lips together as he hesitated, and then leaned forward to kiss her.

While Griffin intended to brush his lips against Jessica's in that magical moment in the moonlight, the car suddenly barreling along the road and swiping them in the headlights killed the mood. Hastily, they stepped further to the side, Griffin catching her elbow as Jessica slipped.

They both laughed a little, and their banter was back.

"Geesh, didn't realize this majestic view was part of a racecourse," quipped Griffin.

"Right," laughed Jessica. Then she shivered.

"Ready to go back?"

"I guess so." Jessica didn't really want to walk away from the magic of this moonlight, but the spell had already been broken. "We can sit in front of the fire with a bottle of wine."

"Absolutely!" agreed Griffin, "And the baklava."

"Oh right, that honey-pastry-whatever you got."

"Uhhuh. Don't worry, once you try it, you'll never forget it. The owners of the pizza place are Greek, like his parents are from the old country, and it's a family recipe. It is sooo good!"

"Ok, ok, I'll try it. I'm more of a chocolate girl, but I'll try it."

"Mmm hmm. You're gonna love it."

In just minutes, they were back at the cabin, stomping the snow off their feet and hanging up their coats.

"I'll stir up the stove, you pour us wine?" offered Jessica.

"Sure."

The mood was cozy as Griffin watched Jessica kneel in front of the stove and stir up the coals, then carefully toss in a couple of pieces of wood. She left the door cracked open so the wood would catch faster and sat back on her heels to watch him.

He laughed as he saw her watching.

"And thees vine here," Griffin spoke with an atrocious accent somewhere between french and italian while hamming up his movements, too, "eees an egceptional vine. De finest of de house! Feerst, we pop the cork." The cork obligingly popped out of the bottle as he said this, "and then ve let eeet brrrreathe for a moment. While eeet do theeeese, ve place de delicate pastrieeees onto de plate. Delactables for de delectable."

By now Jessica was laughing so hard at his antics she could hardly hear the atrocious accent. "I think whatever language you are butchering wants you to please stop, Griffin." She paused for a breath before giggling some more. "I appreciate it, but the wine might run away from that vocal assault."

"Uhh, what, my ahhhhccahnnnnt?"

"Yeah," Jessica rolled her eyes while laughing.

"Fine," Griffin pretended to pout. "I'll just pour the wine and bring over the baklava."

"Ok," giggled Jessica some more. SHe turned back to the stove then to check the fire. Seeing that the smoke had dissipated, and the logs were covered with dancing flames, she shut the small door on the end of the stove and opened up the front wide doors. She then placed the curved screen in front of the open doors, allowing them to enjoy the fire blazing.

She scooted back and leaned against the sofa while still sitting on the floor, her legs stretched out in front of her.

Griffin handed her both glasses and then pulled the coffee table further away so there was room for both of them to sit on the floor.

"Sorry, I do this. I tend to sit on the floor quite often."

"It's because you're an animal person."

"What?"

"You're comfortable on the floor so you can pet the animals."

"There aren't any animals here."

"But if there were, wouldn't you be on the floor petting the dog? Or cat, or whatever."

"Hmm, yeah I guess I would."

"Right."

"Apparently you know me better than I know myself."

"Doubtful. I just know that to be true about me and figured you were the same."

"Ahh. I see."

They sat together in comfortable silence, sipping wine and staring at the flames, arms just barely touching depending how they shifted.

"Oh!" Griffin exclaimed, "baklava!"

"Oh, yeah!"

"Here." he handed her a small plate with a square of sticky pastry on it. "I suppose I could have gotten you a fork, but I just eat it with my fingers. I swear you get sticky either way."

Jessica giggled again, "Ok."

They both used their fingers and took a bite of the sticky layers.

"Oh. My. God." said Jessica, her mouth full.

"Uhhuh, right?" Griffin gave her a knowing look. "I always mean to stop and bring some home, but I never remember to."

"Oh, we'll have to remember to bring some of this. I'll help you to remember this time!"

Griffin watched Jessica lick a crumb from the corner of her mouth and then lick her honey covered fingers. He couldn't help but stare at her very kissable mouth. He smiled, watching her.

Jessica licked the corner of her mouth again. "What?" she asked with a smile.

"You look adorable."

Jessica tucked her bottom lip between her teeth and then leaned forward to him, holding his gaze. Inches away from his lips, she whispered, "You're nuts!" and then laughed out loud.

"Yes, yes, I am. But you're adorable," chuckled Griffin as the sweet mood dissolved, but the warm tension continued to build. "So you're gonna help me remember? We're a team now, I take it."

"Umm, yeah," Jessica murmured, "I guess we are."

"Good." After taking another sip of wine, Griffin asked, "So have you checked your email today to see what kind of package you were offered?" *I have a nice package here available*, snorted Griffin to himself.

"Oh, my god! I haven't checked it since we lost service coming back from Island Pond. He's going to think I'm not interested if he sent me something."

"Or he's going to assume that you have a life and don't just sit by waiting for his email." He put a hand on her leg. "Hush, you're fine. Relax."

Jessica was already pulling out her phone and clicking on the email icon. Griffin watched the messages load, and it seemed like about a hundred of them flew down her screen.

"Geesh, aren't you popular!" he whistled.

"No, not hardly. I bet I just delete about two-thirds of those without even reading them. I swear I unsubscribe from junk every week and yet I still get a ton!"

"Yeah, me too, girl." He kept watching as she clicked next to more messages than not and then deleted a whole swath of them in one swoop.

"Look, here it is." Jessica clicked into the email from Mike. She held it so Griffin could see too. The email itself was brief: *Here's the package I have worked up. If you like it, sign the contract and return it to me at your convenience and we'll figure out your start date and details. You might have to work remotely for a week if I haven't finalized your office space.*

"Umm, I get an office?" Jessica looked at Griffin, eyes wide open.

"Sounds like it."

She then opened the attachment, which was several pages long. The first part was the job description, which completely matched what they had spoken about in the morning except that it added the possibilities for bonus work. The salary was what she had discussed, which still made her grin in excitement. Then she got to the benefits. "Are you kidding me? Full insurance plus gym membership or supplement for health equipment? That's sweet."

"Uhhuh. Some benefits are unexpected, but super cool."

"Like this cell phone with hotspot."

"For when you're working remotely. You'll have a company provided computer, too, obviously."

"Yeah, I see that."

"What's Geraldina's? Why do I have a line of credit there?"

"Ahh, that's a unique benefit to our company. It's the coffee shop downstairs. The owners are friends and barter some things for us. I bet you end up creating some marketing for them, but we all have a credit there. It's handy when you need a midday pick-me-up."

"Sweet!"

"Uhhuh! And they have fantastic soup and sandwiches, too."

"Nice. I usually pack my lunch, but it's good to know there are options."

"You could actually go home for lunch and come back too, if you wanted, or just work mornings, or whatever your little heart desires. You get to almost completely make your own schedule. There will be some times that we all need to be there to work together, but not all that often."

"This is absolutely amazing! Thank you, Griffin!" She leaned over and gave him a quick kiss on the cheek, which absolutely stole his words away. Color bloomed in her cheeks, but couldn't hold her grin at bay.

"You know what we should do now?" asked Griffin when he found his voice again.

"What?"

"We should call that old biddy and give her your notice."

They both laughed.

"No, we won't call her and ruin a perfect day, but we can draft what I'll put in my resignation letter."

"Not as much fun," Griffin tilted his head back and forth, "but sure, could still be fun."

"But we're drafting it in docs so we don't actually send it until sober me can proofread it."

"Why, you think she might fire you?" Griffin laughed again and Jessica giggled, too."

"True. But I can still be professional."

"Probably better for your last week of work, more comfortable."

"Week? I have to give two weeks."

"Well, you don't *have* to. Besides, you have vacation time to use."

"Hmm," Jessica held her lip in her teeth. "I could finish up all my projects, and email my clients to let them know I'm moving on, and be done with all that in about three days. So if we drive back Monday or Tuesday..."

"Exactly. We draft it now. You edit and send it tomorrow. Then next weekend you move into my place."

"Wait, what?"

"Then next weekend you move into my place," repeated Griffin. "I have plenty of room, an extra bedroom. We seem to do alright cooking together." He smiled at her.

"But no, I can find my own place." Jessica was flustered.

"You could, but why? There's parking for us both so we can decide whether to carpool or not, depending on our schedules. And," he had saved this last part for last intentionally, "my place is beach themed rustic decor about a block from the beach. I know that's your style."

"Well it is, but..."

"Uhhuh, no buts."

"Yes, buts"

"Ok, your cute butt at my place."

She couldn't help it. It was so preposterous that she was having this conversation that Jessica just broke down laughing.

"See, the idea grows on you." Griffin could see that he might win this. "Oh, here's this. We'll move you down right away and you can stay with me while you look for another place."

Jessica started nodding her head. She could see the logic of that.

"We'll look," said Griffin, "but housing is rough right now. Finding a decent place at anything near affordable is really hard. I got lucky as it was a fixer-upper when I moved in. So we'll have you stay for a while. We can split rent if that makes you feel better. Or something."

Jessica nodded. "Yeah, that sounds kinda reasonable, actually. It is super helpful of you, too."

"Buuuuut," said Griffin with a grin.

Jessica rolled her eyes. "But what?"

"But you have to cook from scratch at least once a week. Your food is absolutely amazing."

A weight lifted off her shoulders that Jessica didn't even know she had been carrying for so long. This was real, and it was good. "I can do that," she answered with a smile.

"Perfect, it's settled. I have a new roomie." Griffin kept it light, but he was hoping for much more than a roommate.

"Ok, so tell me more about the workplace, the town. What do I need to know?"

"Hmm, that's an entire night of talking." Griffin rubbed his face while he thought. "Ok, there's a bunch of parks, and beaches, and restaurants that I'll show you when we have free afternoons. I bet you'll love the library. It's a gorgeous building with a whole series of rooms that lead to rooms to rooms. They have rooms of books, of course, but then they have little nooks where you can work or read or whatever. I think there are a bunch of groups that meet there each week or month or whatever, too, but I've never joined."

"Umm, ok, The Office. Well, the people are really chill. Except for Mary. She's actually chill too, but she comes across as cold and a hard ass. Just show her your work ethic and she'll come around. She really is nice. Just remember that, because you won't feel it at first. Just be you. The rest of us all work pretty hard most of the time so that sometimes we can just be goofy while we're waiting for inspiration to strike. You'll be allowed to do that even more, I expect, since you're literally in the creative department. Wait, what does that contract say?"

"What do you mean?"

"What does your contract say is your actual job title?"

Jessica flicked on her phone again and scrolled back to the top of the contract to reread it. Her eyes opened wide. "Director of Creative Marketing and Communications."

"Uhhuh, I figured it might be director."

"That doesn't even sound like an actual title."

"Mike probably made it up."

"What?"

"I told you we had just started talking about needing someone. We didn't really have a position yet, like not one that you were filling in replacing someone. So he tailored it to you."

"But director? He hasn't even met me."

"Sure he did. He met you in your interview."

"Yeah, over zoom."

"Yeah, and if you can make a good impression over zoom, imagine how much more amazing you are in person. He knows that. Plus, I said you're cool." Griffin blew on his nails and then buffed them against his chest.

Jessica couldn't help it, but laughed at him again. "Well, damn."

"Yeah, so I don't know what office you'll get. We have some rooms that are open, and Cheri and Magellan were talking about wanting to move into a larger room together since they work together on things 90% of the time and one ends up in the other's office perched over the desk or they take over a conference room. So you might end up with one of theirs. If you do, Cheryl has a magnificent view down to the entrance to a forestry park-like area."

They stayed up late chatting and drinking wine. That night, Jessica went to bed with fewer worries and much more happiness than in a long, long time. She fell asleep with a smile on her face. It couldn't possibly get any better, could it?

Chapter 11 - Day 5 - Monday

"The furnace people should be back today with parts, and then in theory we can leave, right?" Jessica asked over breakfast.

Griffin swallowed the crispy bacon in his mouth and then answered, "Yeah, that's the plan. Not that I really want to rush home and back to work."

"Yeah. The real world beckons," replied Jessica.

They were both a little excited though to return to the real world and move onto the next steps of Jessica finishing out the week at her old job, then moving her out of her old apartment.

"On our way back, I want to stop back at that little store in Littleton. There's something I saw that I want to get."

"Ok, I don't think we're in a rush per se," said Jessica.

"Good. After breakfast we can pack up and then I guess we just wait."

"Yeah. Cause waiting is so much fun!"

"Right."

The furnace guys actually came pretty soon after. And after an hour or two, it was up and running again. They were told that they should let it run for a while 'just to be sure', but they should be all set now. The furnace guys even vacuumed up after themselves. Jessica and Griffin hung out a couple hours after lunch, made sure everything was cleaned up and shipshape. But then they just couldn't handle waiting around anymore.

They eased into a parking space on the side of the street. "You wanna come back in or wait here?" asked Griffin.

"I can just wait, unless you're gonna be awhile."

"Nah. I'll be right back."

"Yeah, I'll just wait."

The crosswalk was behind them, so Jessica didn't bother watching Griffin as he crossed the street and went in. She pulled up a book on her Kindle app and was prepared to chill awhile. However, it was just a couple minutes and Griffin was sliding back into the car and tossing a small bag into the back.

The drive back was uneventful. The further south they went, the more traffic they came across, especially once they hit the Massachusetts line. Nonetheless, the miles sped by as they chatted about music, traveling, favorite snacks, and everything in between.

"You need to stop anywhere before we hit your apartment?" asked Griffin as they pulled into Jessica's town.

"Nah, I have some meals in the freezer and stuff for coffee in the morning. It's all good."

A few minutes later, they were pulling into her driveway. Griffin left the car running, but hopped out to help Jessica carry the stuff up.

"I don't need help. It's fine."

"What kind of friend would I be, then?"

"I don't know, a normal one."

"That's not normal."

"Whatever."

Griffin just laughed while Jessica fished out her keys. She opened the door and set her bag in the hallway, then she turned to grab the bag that Griffin held.

"Uhuh, this first."

"What?"

Griffin kept her bag securely on his shoulder. "I picked this up for you today. You were looking at it when we exploring."

Jessica just blinked at him.

Griffin smiled and slipped a necklace out of the bag. "Here, put it on."

Jessica stood there momentarily dumbfounded. It wasn't an expensive piece of jewelry, under $20, but the fact that he had paid enough attention to remember that she had noticed anything in particular and further that he knew which piece she had gravitated to.

"No. Why would you do that?"

"You liked it. And this way you think of me all week while it rests around your neck."

Together they untangled it from the cardstock it was taped to. Then Jessica slipped the cord over her head. It nestled right in her cleavage. A silver circle with a pentagram in the circle with a green glass, stone centered and around the edges of the scroll of the circle. It was definitely wiccan, and simple, but pretty.

"I love silver, blue, and green," said Jessica.

"I know." Griffin held her eyes. "It suits you."

"Thank you." The words were simple, but Jessica's heart was in full view of him as she uttered the words.

"You're welcome." Griffin leaned forward then and gently kissed Jessica. Their lips pressed together and then their bodies followed as Jessica stretched her arms up around his neck.

Griffin pulled back and rested his forehead against hers.

"You better be busy every night after work packing. I'll be here Saturday morning to help you finish."

"Really?"

"Yes, really." As he moved back, the bag slipped off his shoulder and fell, pushing Jessica back. "Shit, sorry."

"No, it's fine." Jessica bit her lip. "Ok, ummm. Thank you. I'll see you Saturday."

"Good night, Jessica."

"Good night Griffin. I'll miss spending time with you."

Griffin headed to his car. Jessica stepped in and leaned against the door after she closed it. Her fingers held the necklace as she closed her eyes.

She jumped when her phone buzzed. *Start packing, Little Lady. I expect you home by noon on Saturday. ;)*

Jessica grinned.

Chapter 12 - Saturday

The week flew by with Jessica completing all she could at work and leaving helpful directions for whoever would be replacing her. The old biddy might be spiteful and not pass it on, but Jessica could try.

She now had piles of boxes in her living room and hallway, and had donated a bunch of things through a variety of social media groups. She didn't actually need to rush packing, but Griffin made the hurry infectious with his daily texts asking her how many more boxes she had packed. It was difficult to say who was more excited about this next step in her life.

True to his word, Griffin showed up at 8am with large coffees and oversized muffins, something with oatmeal and nuts for him, and cranberry and sugar-topped for Jessica. Jessica just cupped the coffee between her hands and inhaled for a moment, eyes the muffin sitting in a napkin on the table. "Don't talk yet. I know there's lots of work. Just let me enjoy this for a moment."

Griffin chuckled, but obligingly didn't say a word. He did take an enormous bite of his muffin.

Jessica breathed deep again and then sipped the coffee to test how hot it actually was. She moved over then to break off an edge of the muffin top and pop it in her mouth. As she chewed it, she unwrapped the wrapper from the muffin. She always ate the bottom first. The top was the best, and she saved that for last. Griffin watched her with a quirked eyebrow, but still didn't say anything. She looked over at him and laughed. "It's fine. You can talk now. I just needed a moment."

"Nope. That's ok. I'm just watching."

"Uhhuh, whatever. Best for last and all that."

"Ok." Griffin just nodded, like he understood.

"Just go with it."

"I am."

"Ok, so I have a bunch packed up. Some I figure I can donate because I don't actually need it."

"Sure, we don't need two tables."

"I might want a table when I move into my place."

"Hmm, who says you're moving again?"

"You're ridiculous," Jessica laughed again and sipped more coffee.

So, we move the boxes today, and then some furniture tomorrow? And find me a storage unit this afternoon for what doesn't fit in your place."

"Hmm. You probably don't need a storage unit. Depends how much you have." Griffin rubbed a thumb against his cheek. "I have a big shed and don't use all the space. If we actually organize my stuff in there, it's kinda just piled in, then I bet there's enough room for yours."

"Well, not paying for storage would be awesome. Let's look when we get there, yeah?"

"Yup." Griffin looked around. "Muffins first. Then boxes to the back of the truck. I have a tarp to put over them, then straps, just in case. Then plants, and your kitchenware weird shaped things in the back seat? Well, some plants and some kitchenware. I bet you have a bunch of both."

Jessica bit her lip. "I do. Is that ok?"

"Damn girl, the way you cook, if you want to bring the whole dang sink, I'll make that happen. "Griffin grinned at her, "Plants are good too. If there's not enough room at the house, then we'll bring them to the office."

"Yeah, some of them just came from my desk at work. They just need weekend housing from you and they can go to my new-work space."

"Uhhuh, unless I like them."

"Oh yeah? You're kidnapping my plants?"

"Maybe."

"Oh, ok. Just so we're clear." Jessica finished the bottom of her muffin and now just had the giant sugar crystal laden top left."

"You're just saving the sugar for last," quipped Griffin.

"Not exactly. Well, yes. But I would do the same without the sugar on top."

"Uhhuh."

"Pumpkin doesn't have sugar on top, neither does chocolate. I do it with those, too."

"Uhhuh."

"If you like muffins, I can make them each week. I have an awesome recipe and some of that weird sized kitchenware if an oversized-muffin pan."

"The pan is over sized or the muffins are."

She gave him a withering look.

"I mean," he held up his hands, "I just have a normal sized oven."

"C'mon, let's start this crap." Jessica propped open her door and picked up a box.

Griffin watched her cute ass as she moved out the door, then he picked up a box and followed. He could not wait to have her moved into his house!

The clinking of dishes and the thud of furniture being disassembled echoed the tangible shift in their lives. A picture appeared in the kitchen of the two of them, plus Mellie as teenagers.

"Oh. My. God." Griffin picked up the small framed photo and stared. "Good god we were young, weren't we?"

Jessica laughed, "We were. And you were a pain in the ass! You were always a pest trying to get our attention, playing so many pranks on us."

"Well, you coulda just let me join you."

"Yeah, like we enjoyed any of the same things then beyond s'mores and soda."

"It was a good summer, though. You let me tag along to a street fair. Is that what this is from?"

"I'm not sure. That was my first thought, but there was a carnival that summer too, so I'm not sure."

"We'll have to ask Mellie. She's coming over tomorrow."

"She is?" asked Jessica, sitting up straight from where she had dropped over the island. "Yeah, a lot of times we grill and hang out one day of the weekend. Summertime we hang at the beach. Wintertime, I still grill, but we hang out in the living room."

"Did you tell her I was staying here for a while?"

Griffin raised his eyebrows. "You didn't tell her you were moving in?"

"I actually haven't." Jessica bit her lip, "I wasn't avoiding her, but after letting her know I made it back home safe, I've just been super busy and we haven't really chatted."

"Huh."

Jessica giggled. "Should we tell her?"

"Or just let her be surprised when she walks in?" Griffin laughed, "She'll hate us. She might never forgive us."

"Noo, she won't be mad."

"She won't *not* be mad."

"Hmm."

"Just tell her I'm bringing broccoli salad, and don't let on anything else."

"You're a mean one, Ms Grinch!"

"Ha! You have no idea!"

"Hmm. Good to know. Wait, broccoli salad. What the hell is that?"

"Oh, it's sooo good. It has bacon in it."

"Sold. That's all I need to know."

"Right."

"Oh, that's right. We need to grab the crock pot from the fridge. It's all ready to plug in at your place-"

"-our place."

"-yeah. So that way we can eat later."

"Oh yeah, that's thinking ahead. What have you made us?"

"Don't worry, it's be something terrible."

"Ha! I doubt that."

"Hmm."

"You won't tell me?"

"I'm a mean one, remember?"

Griffin just scoffed, but went along with the game. "Fine. I'll grab it. We should be able to put it on the floor in the backseat and wedge it pretty well so it won't tip."

"Perfect."

After the second trip of hauling in a truckload of boxes, they were both pooped.

"I'm not actually sure what you have in that crock pot of magic, Little Lady, but it smells amazing.

"Awww, thanks." Jessica smiled shyly at the compliment and at being called Little Lady. She had never had a cute nickname. "I have to say," she slumped down on the couch, "that I am really content to be done for the day. We don't need to move it all today or even this weekend. I have plenty to get me through the week."

"I really wanted to get it done today," Griffin held up his hand as she started to argue, "but I'm ready to admit defeat. We can do another load tomorrow."

"Thank god!"

"Beer time."

"Oh, definitely!"

"Look, I even stocked your Downeast cider. Good grief, there are a lot of flavors. I had no idea which you liked, so I just got the original."

"Yeah! The original is fine. There was a jalapeno one a couple of years ago that I loved. If you ever see that, buy like a case of it."

Griffin quirked an eyebrow. "Really? Jalapeno?"

"Yeah! The pumpkin is my second favorite, but it's a fall flavor."

"Which others?"

"I like most of them. There was some blue raspberry or something that I really hated, but most of the others are decent. Maybe not the strawberry. There was something like that which was less than great. Except for that blue thing, even the bad ones are decent and the good ones are excellent."

"Hmm, duly noted."

They sat together in silence, sipping from their cold cans for a moment. Just comfortable and resting muscles.

"We can't sit too long, or I'm just going to stiffen up," said Jessica.

"I know," sighed Griffin.

"Ok, so can we just move some boxes into the room you're graciously loaning me, and we can stack the others outside the door for me to unpack through the week?"

"Sure."

"We did a bunch of the hard stuff earlier with all the ones already in your shed."

"That's right, only like half that first load needs to be moved now, huh?" Griffin sat up with renewed energy then. "Ok, we got this."

"Yup."

Griffin reached a hand down and pulled Jessica up. "Ok, let's finish up and then I get first shower while you unpack your unmentionables and what not."

Jessica laughed along with him, "Deal!"

Jessica looked around her new room. It was beautiful. It was larger than her old apartment's space, almost that old bedroom and livingroom combined. Plus, with the beach and rustic decor, it was all bright and white with accents in her favorite colors. You could look around and just imagine the salt air blowing in through the curtains. You know, if they were open, and it wasn't wintertime.

Jessica giggled to herself and then pushed a box across the floor to the white dresser in the corner by the sink. It was interesting having a sink and vanity right in the bedroom. There was a bathroom just off the bedroom too, with a shower and toilet. Having the sink separate was a little odd, but having her clothes right next to the mirror and such was handy.

She made quick work of putting away her clothes and breaking down those boxes. She laid out her phone charge, water bottle, glasses, and stuff on the bookshelf beside the bed. She laid her laptop on the ottoman by the chair beside the window seat. She had always wanted a window seat.

It seemed like Griffin was making all sorts of her dreams come true. She lived a short walk from the beach now. She had a dream job, a gorgeous house to live in, and a truly sweet guy paying attention to her. Like really paying attention; he knew how she liked her coffee even. Griffin had grown up and now he seemed like the most amazing guy. He was almost book boyfriend material. They had talked a little about his hopes and dreams, but now she realized he had kept steering the conversation back to her. She knew he loved this house, that he liked his job, that he wanted to settle down with somebody to have fun with, but not a family yet...what else did she know? She knew his family, obviously. She and Mellie had been friends for almost two decades. Speaking of which, what was Mellie gonna say? Jessica didn't think she would be upset, but would she get weirded out? And she hadn't even talked to her this week; she hadn't gone to their gym days. Time to send a text.

Jessica: Oh my god, I have had such a crazy week. I'm so glad I get to see you and catch up!

Mellie: Hey! I thought maybe you were sick or something, you've been so quiet. But then Griffin said you'll be at his house tomorrow???

Jessica: Yeah, that's one of those things to talk about. I got a new job because of him. I'll tell you all about it tomorrow.

Mellie: Really? Where? Doing what?

...

Mellie: Jessica? I don't like secrets! What job? Where?

Mellie: Jessica!?

...

Mellie: You're a brat!

Jessica laughed as she plugged in her phone, ignoring Mellie's frustration. She stripped off her dirty clothes and had just wrapped up in a thick towel when she suddenly heard Griffin.

"What did you say to her?" he yelled out.

Jessica laughed. She finished pulling her hair into a bun, then cracked her door open. "I just texted her that I had a lot to tell her, like that you had gotten me a new job." She grinned. "Then I stopped answering her."

"You're the deplorable one," Griffin laughed too. He held out his phone so she could see the screen. "Now she's blowing up *my* phone." His eyes roved over her obviously naked body, wrapped up in a thick towel. He smiled devilishly. "Very nice. I'm glad she's not here right now."

Jessica blushed scarlet and was flustered beyond words. She noticed his brown curls were still damp, and he looked completely relaxed in a gray t-shirt and black lounge pants. He stalked towards her.

"Nope!" Jessica whirled, almost losing her towel, and closed the door between them. "My turn for a shower," she called through the door.

"You're mean!" Griffin couldn't help but grin. *What was this between them?* They hadn't even slept together, except to sleep together, and she was moved into his house and driving him wild. "Fine," he called out. "I'll be down watching tv when you care to join."

"Ok," Jessica called back and then bit her lip. *What was this?*

Chapter 13 - Sunday

Saturday night had been spent cuddling on the couch drinking red wine, with the tv on, and both of them reading. They were relaxed and just so comfortable together. Eventually, it had gotten late and moving had tuckered them out. Their beds were calling to them. They walked up the stairs together with tension building.

"I don't want to rush you," said Griffin quietly, "but you're welcome in my room anytime."

Jessica was so flustered, she couldn't find any words. Griffin sealed it with a gentle kiss and then a gentle push towards her room. It took all of his self-control to do so. He watched her slip into her room, turning back to close the door with a sweet blush and a lip caught between her teeth.

"G'night," she whispered.

"Goodnight, Jessica."

The next morning, after a cold shower, Griffin met Jessica in the kitchen early. She had bacon and eggs going, so he popped slices of wheat toast into the toaster. Small talk was easy from how quickly they fell asleep to agreeing to move just one load of boxes and furniture today, so they could relax before Mellie came. "We'll need a quick trip to the store for today. What about groceries for the week, too?"

"Ugh," groaned Jessica, "Yeah, I should do some food prep for lunches, too. You said you usually pack your lunches, right?"

"Usually. It's cheaper."

"So how about we prep together a couple of my favorites and a couple of yours?"

"Yeah, sure. I rarely eat much for breakfast during the week, but pack a couple fruit or protein snacks, then a lunch meal."

"Really? Me too. Perfect." Jessica grinned. It was almost like a fated mates kind of thing from her fantasy books, how similar they were.

So responsible adults they were, they traveled back to Jessica's apartment, loaded her favorite comfy chair and a little chest, and a bunch of boxes. At the last minute, she saw her travel mug by the sink. "Oh shit, that's right. I washed this Friday night and didn't pack it. I need this for Monday morning."

"Yes, coffee is the elixir of gods before going to work on a Monday."

Looking at the lack of room, they agreed to unload apartment things before going to the grocery store.

"We're running out of time, let's hurry," said Jessica. "We can just pile these here, until later, but we need to get the food to prep before Mellie gets here."

"I hate rushing," groaned Griffin. "But you're right. Let's go."

Mellie arrived at her brother's place just after noon, to see Jessica comfortably working in Griffin's kitchen. Mellie saw the famous broccoli salad, next to a plate of marinated steak tips ready to cook. Jessica was filling travel containers with slices of apple and cheese.

Mellie lifted an eyebrow at Jessica, and Griffin just laughed, handing her a beer.

"Come in, my dear sister."

"Why thank you, dear brother." Mellie slipped off her boots next to a stack of boxes with Jessica's familiar handwriting on them. She laid her coat on top of the closest boxes.

"Ok my dear brother and best friend," Mellie walked to the kitchen where Jessica was working and set down a bowl of chocolate looking desert. "You seem to have some splaining to do."

"Hi Mellie," said Jessica with a smile.

"Oh, don't 'hi Mellie' me. You two have been keeping secrets. Just what happened in Vermont, anyway?"

"Well, quite a lot."

"Apparently."

"Oh, don't be mad, Mels," cajoled Griffin.

"Mad? Are you daft? It appears that my best friend and my brother have just connected in a whole new way and maybe at some future point my best friend might become my sister for realsies. I'm not mad about that. But why didn't you tell me?!" She glared across the counter at Jessica and punched Griffin in the shoulder."

The tension evaporated out of the room, and they all laughed.

"Tell me just what the hell happened between you two."

"Well..."

"Um, well, I did listen to you to give her space at first," said Griffin at the same time.

"Wait, what?" Jessica demanded.

"Nevermind," said Griffin to Jessica, "I can tell you later."

"No, it's alright," interrupted Mellie, "He was looking all jealous and moody when you were flirting with that guy at the bar and I told him to leave you be."

"No, you told me she needed a one-night stand sort of fling."

"I did actually," admitted Mellie. "Is that what this is?"

"I don't think so," Jessica bit her lip after answering.

"No, not if I have a say in it."

"Have you slept together yet?"

"No!"

Griffin amended that, "Well, technically we slept together," Jessica groaned, "but literally we were sleeping, that's it."

"So you were in the same bed, all platonic, and slept. Uhhuh." Mellie did not sound convinced.

"More or less," answered Jessica.

"I did wake up with a wicked hard-on."

"Yes, you did." They all laughed again.

"We need beer." Mellie went to the fridge and put the case in that she had brought and took out two cold beers and a cold cider. "He even has your brand? Or did you stock this?" She looked knowingly at Jessica.

"Yeah, he bought it for me. He's very observant, your brother."

"Hmm." She sipped the beer, then narrowed her eyes. "Wait a minute, you teased me with something about a new job. What new job?"

"Hmm, I did mention that, didn't I?"

"Yeah. And then you just stopped texting me because you're a brat!"

"Yeah, well, Griffin got me a job at his company."

"Oh no, I didn't!" interrupted Griffin. "You got that job for yourself. All I did was connect you to an interview for a job I knew about."

"Details, people," demanded Mellie.

"Yeah, so Griffin heard me talking to my supervisor-"

"The biyatch."

"Yeah, and she was in full throttle. So he eventually convinced me that I should work somewhere less abusive."

Mellie threw her hands up. "I've been telling you that for months!"

"Yeah, you have," admitted Jessica. "But he also knew of a writing job with flexible hours that his company was about to post."

"And I hooked her up with an interview with Mike."

"Oooh," Mellie winced. "He's tough to interview with."

"Really? He seemed really nice."

"Oh, he's a great guy, but this company is his baby. He's ruthless in interviews," clarified Mellie.

Griffin grinned, "He loved her. Sent her an awesome offer the same day. We drafted her two weeks notice that night."

"So you still have another week in your old job?"

"Nope. This is a vacation week. I'm done. And I start this new gig on Monday."

"In her own office," added Griffin.

"What?! Awesome!" Mellie swept Jessica into an enormous hug. "Good, girl, you have earned that!"

Griffin preened and rubbed his fingers against his chest. "I did good, didn't I?"

"Yes, you Lummox, you did good," laughed Mellie. "Now tell me all the deets. Not just the job, but all of...this." She waved her hand at the two smiling goofballs and the boxes while she spoke.

"Well," Jessica bit her lip. "I don't really know how this happened. Not really."

In a moment of seriousness, Griffin nodded. "Yeah, it wasn't like a plan or anything. We just happen to fit together well. We seem to like the same things, and drink a lot of wine, and just relax near each other."

"Yeah, even shoveling the driveway with you was kinda fun," laughed Jessica.

Mellie just looked from one to the other and drank her beer.

"I mean, I'm not keeping secrets from you. You know I tell you everything-"

"*Almost* everything, apparently."

"Ok, almost everything," agreed Jessica with a smile. But there wasn't like a big moment, we just did. I don't know."

"Well, I think it 'started' if you will," Griffin air quoted while he spoke, "the day we brought them to the rental. You and I walked around Littleton and just hung out."

"True. I guess that is when it all just started feeling comfy and we ended up talking all day about everything and nothing."

"And we drank a lot of wine."

"Yeah, that too. Then we spent the entire weekend just hanging out, waiting for the furnace repairs."

"-Which is how I talked you into applying for the job."

"Yeah, we even hung out working. And you convinced me to interview for this job that hadn't even been posted yet, and well, here we are."

"A little more than that. You cooked for me too."

"We took turns."

"Yeah, but you cook *really* well. Even the lady at the grocery store said I should keep you."

"What lady?" Jessica was completely confused.

"Remember, we were in line and you told me you cook Indian, too. The check out lady said I needed to keep you."

"Ohhhh, right." Jessica blushed scarlet.

"I see." Mellie just laughed at her best friend's discomfort. "So you spent the whole weekend alone, snowed or iced in, and didn't even sleep together."

"Nope." Griffin grinned. "You should be proud of me."

Mellie snorted, and Jessica turned a new shade of scarlet.

"It was cool," Jessica tried to change the subject. "We found some journals and letters on the bookshelf. I guess they were your grandparents' and they were snowed in together the weekend they met."

"Really? I thought they met selling cows or something."

"Yeah, your grandfather and his dad were selling cows, but they stopped to visit with your great grandparents and were iced in."

"Grams saved at least some of his letters to her while he was in college and what not. It was pretty cool to read."

"Aww," teased Mellie, "two new lovers falling in love reading love letters."

Chapter 14 - Monday

Jessica woke up Monday morning bright and early before her alarm even went off. Truthfully, she had woken up several times, anxious of oversleeping. Silly, but true. She showered to calm her mind and relax her body. She was feeling a little better by the time she went downstairs. Griffin smiled up at her and poured coffee into her travel mug.

"Ready for your first day?"

"Honestly, I'm nervous as hell."

"Yeah, I probably would be too." He smiled gently, "And it probably wouldn't help me, roles reversed, but you have nothing to be nervous about. We know you can rock the work, so what's the worst that can possibly happen? You forget someone's name? Big deal." He slid her mug over. He had slipped a piece of chocolate on top of it while talking.

Jessica giggled and relaxed a little. "Yeah, you're right. I'm still anxious, though." She unwrapped the piece of chocolate and popped it in her mouth.

"Yeah, you'll be great, though."

"Hmm," she took a deep breath. "Yeah, we'll see."

"You'll be great. C'mon."

Today they drove to work, even though they could have walked. It was winter and not that nice out. The quick drive brought butterflies back to Jessica's stomach.

Griffin looked over. "Breathe," he said.

"Yeah." They parked, and Jessica took a deep breath through her nose. "Ok, let's do this."

"Thatta girl," Griffin grinned at her. "Let's go find Mike and see if your office is bigger than mine."

"I thought you knew which office is mine."

"Well, I'm pretty sure, but not positive. Let's go find out."

Jessica grabbed her bag and gripped her coffee as they walked in.

"Want me to give you a running commentary of everyone we pass, or save it for later?"

"Just hit me with the most important people for now."

"Yup. Well, first up is Jerry here," Griffin grinned at Jerry and saluted him with his cup. "He is the most important man in the building."

"Naw man," laughed Jerry.

"Don't listen to him. Most. Important. Man. In the building." Griffin laughed and kept them walking, but spoke loudly, "If you need anything, he's in charge of the maintenance and safety of the building. Between him and our secretaries, they can fix anything or find anything you need."

"Ahhh," Jessica understood and called back over her shoulder as Griffin ushered her into the elevator, "Pleased to meet you, Jerry!"

"Now when we get out, there will probably be a few people kinda standing around and visiting at the welcome desk. We kinda gather there first thing sometimes and chat. Just walk in like you belong because you DO belong."

"Yeah." The elevator dinged and slowly opened.

"Hey guys, this is my friend Jessica. She's our new copywriter. I'm not going to tell her all your names because, face it, that's too overwhelming." And just like that everyone laughed and related to Jessica as the new person overwhelmed and the whole mood was relaxed as they surrounded her with "Welcome aboard!" "Good to meet you, Jessica!" and a silly voiced "Oooh, new blood."

Griffin steered her around the corner and presumably towards Mike's office.

"Whew," Jessica huffed a moment, "Thank you for that. It could have been really awkward."

"I live to serve," grinned Griffin. He had actually enjoyed watching everyone seeing Jessica for the first time. "Stop here for a moment," Griffin motioned to a door to their right. "Let me drop my stuff. This is my office, by the way."

"I assumed," replied Jessica dryly.

"Yeah, sorry." Griffin dropped his bag on his desk, but kept his coffee. "Just down here is Mike's office. He likes to be at the end, so he can walk past our offices and check in each day."

"That makes sense," she nodded.

"Yeah, he's a good boss." Griffin knocked on the partially closed door at the end of the hall on the left.

"Ahh, you must be Jessica!" The voice was friendly and matched the face of the middle-aged man behind the desk. He quickly stood up and came around the desk to shake Jessica's hand. His grip was firm and warm. He was tall, and she had to look up to meet his sparkling green eyes. "Welcome aboard!"

Griffin dropped into a chair in front of the desk and slurped his coffee.

"Morning, Griff," added Mike.

Jessica laughed, instantly at ease. "Pleased to meet you."

"Please sit. Make yourself comfortable. It's what most people do." He looked pointedly at Griffin. Griffin just grinned. Jessica realized he was almost always grinning and laughing. His entire demeanor was like a happy golden retriever.

"Ok Griffin, I take it you want to stay to make sure I'm nice?"

"Yeah, just moral support until you need to talk money stuff. That's between the two of you."

"Why?" asked Jessica. "You already saw the offer and watched me sign it."

"Yeah, but I don't need to know anything else like that. That's your private stuff."

"Right," said Mike, looking between them, "and I assume that you've described the building to her and a little about our normal days."

"Kinda a barebones bit. Obviously enough to sell her on it."

"Hmm. Ok, well, let's start by showing you your office. Your laptop and phone should be there."

"Phone?"

"Yeah, I decided that you should have a company phone if you'll be working out of the office half the time."

"Hey," interjected Griffin, "how come I don't get a phone?"

"You want one?"

"Yeah. Of course."

"Really?"

"Well," Griffin sipped his coffee, "let me think about it."

"Uhhuh. So, I think it works out well that the office I want to give you happens to be right across from Griffin's, so if you have questions, he's right there."

"Sweet. Being near him will be good. Thank you."

"Well, don't thank me yet. He can be quite the prankster."

"Hey now!"

"Yeah, I know." Jessica couldn't help but roll her eyes.

"That's right, I forgot you two grew up together. Has he always been a pain in the ass?"

"Yeah," Jessica grinned at Griffin, "but he grows on you."

"Yeah," agreed Mike, "we rather like him. Most of the time."

"Thank you, I think."

Mike led the way, and they walked back down the hall. "Here you go," he held open the door.

Light streamed through the window onto a hardwood floor and a gorgeous cobalt blue rug. On the cherry wood desk sat a sleek laptop and a small green plant. "I think having a plant helps bring life into a room," offered Mike. "If you don't want it or don't like lemongrass, I'll take it back, but it's my little welcome gift to you."

"Aww, thanks! I love plants."

"You do?" asked Griffin.

"Yeah."

"Great, I'll let you settle in. Griffin, bring her down to get her id taken soon ok, that way it can be printed for her by this afternoon?"

"Sure thing, boss."

Mike turned back to her. "You'll need that stupid piece of plastic for everything. Ok kids, I'll talk to you later. Griffin, try to get some work done today, ok? Once you're settled, check your email. Griff will show you how. There are some projects we talked about. Wander around the building, play around with the projects and get comfortable today. I won't start cracking the whip until tomorrow. Take today to get a feel for us."

"Ok," Jessica bit her lip. The butterflies were back and caught in a hurricane in her belly. "Thank you."

"Thank you, Jessica. Welcome to the team!"

Mike left, and Griffin closed the door behind him. There was a window into the hall, but the blind was already closed. Griffin swooped in and gave Jessica a hug. He leaned in and whispered, "Welcome to the team. I'm really glad you're here."

"Thanks," answered Jessica softly.

Staring into her eyes, Griffin wanted to do nothing more than hold her tight and then cuddle up on a couch and work together, just like they had in Vermont. Instead, he gave her a quick kiss on the lips and stepped back. "Ready for a tour, or do you want to sit here for a few first?"

Jessica was focussed more on her tingling lips than the question, but pulled her focus back. "Umm, I kinda want to pull open my email, and get a feel for the room, then have you show me around."

"Great, let's get you signed in and then I'll leave you be for a half hour while I check mine. When you're ready, come grab me."

"Yeah, sounds good." The butterflies had calmed down again. With luck, they would just calmly flutter the rest of the day.

The day flew by and Jessica met so many people she was pretty sure her head might explode with any more new names. But, while overwhelming, it was also an overwhelmingly welcoming environment. This was not what Jessica was used to, and through the day, her shoulders kept tightening, waiting for the other shoe to drop.

Jessica was enjoying the project she was working on and thought, *How is this even possible? Three weeks ago, I was in a miserable job and with a douchebag of a boyfriend. Now I have a dream job, I love this project, and am free to do whatever I want in my free time. Griffin is sweet, and the house is great. The ocean is so close...*

The gentle knocking on the doorframe startled her. Looking up, Jessica smiled when she saw Griffin standing there.

"Ready to knock off?" he asked.

"Wait, really? Already?"

"Honey, it's 3:30."

"Holy shit."

"Lost track of time, huh? Good thing I'm here to save you," chuckled Griffin.

"Yeah, Usually I'm watching the clock to see how soon I can escape." Jessica laughed too.

"Ok, you working here tomorrow or do you need to bring things home?"

"No, I was planning on working here for the week. Get a better feel for the team, etc."

"Nice." Griffin was happy with that. *I knew she was a perfect fit for the company.* "Grab your coat then, and bag and let's go."

"Yeah, give me a moment to finish this thought."

"Ok, I'll meet you downstairs then. I want a coffee. You want one?"

Jessica bit her lip. Coffee would be nice, but the coffee at home was perfectly fine and far cheaper.

"You have a tab, remember, with a certain amount free. If you go over that, you pay it, but it should last you all month with a coffee a day and a couple lunches."

"Yeah, ok. I would love a mocha latte."

"One mocha latte coming up."

"Thanks. I just need a couple of minutes."

"Take your time."

Jessica typed out another paragraph pretty quickly and bulleted the next ideas for tomorrow. It was all done on the cloud, but she did a back up save to her flash drive and dropped that in her bag. Then she scooped up her stuff and stepped out of the office, closing her door behind her. She stood there a moment with her hand on the handle, grateful for the day. Turning, she hurried down to meet Griffin.

She stepped into the elevator next to a guy in a green polo and khaki shorts. She blinked, but went with it. New Englanders were weird when it came to cold and it must have worked for him.

He obviously looked her up and down, but not in a creepy way. Jessica could feel the heat in her cheeks.

"Hey, you must be the new girl. The writer."

"Yeah," Jessica bit her lip. "Yeah, I guess that's me."

"Good, Hey I'm Jonas. Welcome aboard!"

"Thanks."

"Like it so far?"

"Yeah, I really do. I'm a little overwhelmed, but it's good."

He popped a red lollypop in his mouth and held one out to her. Jessica shook her head. He grinned at her while rolling the lollypop around his mouth. He tipped his head, grinned and said, "If you need a hand or want someone to show you around, I'm happy to help. Jonas, at your service." He bowed and swept out a hand as the elevator dinged and slowly opened.

Griffin was leaning against the wall. He smiled and held out her cup as she stepped out.

"I think I'm set, thanks Jonas," said Jessica, smiling at Griffin.

"Aww man, I see how it is. You work fast, Griff." He popped the red lollypop out of his mouth and winked.

"Nah man, break a leg," laughed Griffin. "But she has higher standards than you."

Jessica lifted her eyebrows but didn't say anything as she took the paper cup of liquid heaven. Griffin locked arms with her and they walked out. Griffin looked over his shoulder and called, "Goodbye Jonas, enjoy the afternoon. I'll enjoy mine."

Jessica waited until they were out of sight and then punched him in the arm. "You're awful."

"Yeah, he's not a bad guy, but if you don't shut him down, he will aggressively flirt with you every day. Up to you, though."

"Nah, I'm good. Thanks."

Chapter 15 - Friday

Life quickly became a routine and the first week flew by at work. Jessica was confident in her abilities there. Home life was good, too. Sometimes there was a moment of awkwardness but most of the time they were completely comfortable. They continued to talk about anything and everything and shared a few sweet kisses here and there. They each did little sweet and considerate things for each other. She continued to cook foods she knew he liked; he gave her a shoulder rub each night. It was a happy rhythm. But the sexual tension was growing.

Friday came, and Jessica was flying high with new friends who actually appreciated her ideas and her attitude. At lunch, some new friends stopped by her office. She heard them talking to Griffin and then they stopped by to see her.

"You wanna join us for drinks after work tonight?"

"Umm, maybe."

"There's a cute little bar and pizza place just around the corner. We usually just walk over for a few drinks and to chatter for a couple of hours. Maybe we'll order some food, at least a couple of apps to share."

"Um, yeah, I guess so. Come grab me when you're ready."

"Sure thing, Girl!"

The afternoon flew by. The girls stopped by. "You ready?"

"Umm, I can be."

"Great, the others will join us over there. It's not anything formal."

"Cool." Jessica closed her laptop and scooped her files together and stacked it all neatly. She slid it into her bag and slung it over her shoulder. She peeked into Griffin's office. He was on the phone, but mouthed, "You headed for drinks?" She nodded yes. "I'll see you later," he mouthed back.

She smiled and gave a little wave. She met the girls by the elevator and then they walked around the corner. As soon as they turned the corner, Jessica saw the place. Drinks and laughs soon ruled the afternoon and Jessica really got to know her coworkers now that they were out of the workplace. More people showed up, but never Griffin.

Eventually, Jessica and another girl were ready to leave. Jessica bit her lip as she considered the walk home. She didn't really relish it. She didn't mind the dark, but she wasn't a fan of walking dark streets alone. Luckily, one of the others, Jennifer, saw her hesitation. "That's right, you usually ride in with Griffin, don't you? Need a ride?"

"No, it's fine." Jessica answered quickly.

"Really?" Jennifer lifted an eyebrow.

"Well..."

"Uhhuh. I'll give you a ride. C'mon."

It was just a quick drive, so Jessica agreed. "Well, if you don't mind, I could use a ride."

"Of course!"

They kept chattering as they left and for the quick car ride.

"Thank you so much!" said Jessica as she got out.

"Of course! I would never want someone to have to walk home in the dark. If it had still been afternoon, I might have left you, but not at this time."

"Thank you."

Jessica quietly slipped into the house. She had a quick glass of water and then climbed the stairs as quietly as she could. She dropped her bag off on her bed and slipped out of her clothes. She slid on a fresh thong and t-shirt, and hesitated. This was the perfect opportunity, but she was suddenly nervous. The alcohol gave her a little liquid courage. She stepped back into the hall. She hesitated again and then walked down to Griffin's room. She stepped in and then slid quietly into his bed.

"Hey," he said quietly, as he lifted up the blankets for her to slide in.

"Hey," she said. She snuggled up against him so they were spooning. His warmth against her back felt amazing.

Griffin slipped an arm around her.

"I thought you were coming out for drinks too?"

"Nah, not really my scene."

"No?"

"No."

"I wouldn't have gone then, but I thought you were coming."

"Why?" he asked. "You're not tied to me."

"No, but I like to be with you."

"You're sweet."

"No, you are."

"And now you're here. In my bed."

"Yeah," she bit her lip again. "I am."

"Are you biting your lip in that adorable way you have?"

"Ummm, maybe."

"Of course you are."

Jessica laughed softly, and so did Griffin. He pulled her tighter against him and she sighed in contentment. "This feels right."

Griffin kept his arm around Jessica with her pressed up against him. He had no idea how this happened, but he didn't want it to end.

He hadn't been surprised when she decided to join the girls for drinks. It was a weekly thing they did, but he just found it exhausting. Nor did he enjoy the gossip that happened about half the time. He didn't begrudge Jessica going, but he was disappointed not to spend the evening with her. He had gotten used to their banter and liked having her home with him.

When the jerk earlier this week had hit on her in the elevator, he realized that he did actually want her all to himself. But he would never force her to do that. He never wanted her to feel the least bit obligated, and he was already nervous that she would feel a bit obligated because he led her to the job and she lived in his house. He wanted a genuine relationship, not one that was ever tinged with doubt that she was with him because she felt she owed him.

Still, he was disappointed that she didn't ask if he was going out for drinks before deciding. When he heard her come home, he relaxed, glad that she was safe and sound. It was silly; she was a grown adult, but he still worried. They had ridden in together in one car because he had forgotten about the weekly drinks. He was going to walk home and leave her the car, but she had already left. So he came home. His home that he loved, that then felt completely empty and lonely.

He listened to her come up the stairs and go to her room. He thought about calling out goodnight, but that seemed to border on creepy, and he decided not to.

Imagine his surprise then when his bedroom door opened, and she came in. Once it was apparent that she was climbing into bed with him, he was more than willing to hold open the blanket and invite her in close. He was completely surprised that she was there. In. his. Bed. But he was more than willing for her to snuggle up against him. Draping his arm over her and pulling her tight felt perfect.

"This feels right," said Jessica.

"Uhhuh, it sure does," agreed Griffin.

Jessica scooted forward ever so slightly and then slipped her right hand between them. She rubbed him through his boxers. Griffin groaned.

"I'm nervous, y'know," she said.

"God, I can't tell that."

"No, not right now. Well, not much right now."

Griffin could almost hear her biting her lip.

"No, I mean, I'm afraid of screwing us up. It feels so good together. Us. I don't want to rush and screw things up."

"Hmm, I get that." Griffin spoke softly against her ear, and then kissed her neck. "We are good together. We fit."

"Yeah, like I enjoy every moment I spend with you. I don't want to lose this feeling. You make me happy and I don't even know how. I'm afraid to start a relationship with you, y'know, and screw it up and lose this, too."

Right at that moment, just spooning felt perfect, but her hand was also driving him wild. He started to roll away as he said, "I don't want you to rush anything. For *us* to rush anything. I don't want to lose this either. I don't want to lose you."

As he had pulled away, Jessica had made a no sound and reached back further to tug him back against her.

"It's easier to talk sometimes about the big stuff, when we're in a dark room and just beside each other. I don't know, maybe it's because you can't see my face."

He moves away again, but keeps his hand on her and then began to rub her back. Almost like soothing a skittish horse.

"Well, I'm always willing to talk out the big stuff while laying in bed." They both chuckled a little. "But to completely concentrate, you should probably wear more clothes. When you're ready, if you're ever ready, I just want to feel more of your skin pressing against my skin."

Taken out of context, it could have been the creepiest thing to say, but in that moment, Jessica felt all the sweetness that was intended.

"Ok."

Griffing brought his arm up around her again, and they moved back to spooning closely.

JESSICA WOKE UP WITH Griffin's arm still holding her protectively against him. She didn't move, relishing his warmth and the smell of him in the blanket around her face.

"It's Saturday. We don't have to get up."

Blissfully, Jessica considered Griffin's words. She didn't really want this feeling to end. But, being an adult and all, she also knew they had stuff to do. It became even harder to leave as she felt his morning hardness against her back and felt an ache to answer it.

"I know, but we do have stuff to do."

"It can wait."

"Hmm." Seizing her courage, she continued, "As to waiting, I was thinking..."

Unconsciously, Griffin's arm tightened around her as if to keep from losing her.

"See, I'm afraid of rushing us into a relationship, and screwing it up, and then losing this amazingness we have."

"Uhhuh, but-"

"Hush," Jessica interrupted. "So I'm afraid and I want to take it slowly, but, I, ...I also don't want to wait." She scooted forward just a bit and slipped her hand back to caress him.

Griffin groaned at the heat of her hand as she caressed him. "Oh God, Jessica-"

"Hush," Jessica said again. "So I was thinking we're consenting adults so we could figure out a friends with benefits sort of relationship while I get settled here. More settled here," she amended. "And we could start dating. Like some actual dates, not necessarily like dinner and a movie dates, but times specifically set as a date to hang out and get to know each other more."

"Oh, um," Griffin shook his head to clarify his thoughts. But it was difficult with Jessica's very warm and very talented hand stroking him, and he just wanting to roll her onto her back and kiss her deeply. "You need to stop that for a moment so I can focus." Jessica stopped stroking, but she didn't remove her hand.

"OK, so basically you're saying we should sleep together now, and maybe occasionally, but we continue actively growing our relationship deeper. Is that it?"

"I, um, yeah. Pretty much."

"How could I possibly say no to that?" Griffin gave a throaty laugh. "But I'll wait. I don't want to, but we can wait until you're absolutely sure. I don't want you to feel rushed. I want us to be solid for the rest of our lives."

Jessica bit her lip. He was such a gentleman, and she knew exactly how much he didn't want to wait. The proof was literally in her hand.

"No, I want you right now. But I also want to keep getting to know you more. Intentionally building *us* more."

Griffin did roll her over then and hovered just over her face, lips almost touching. "If you're sure, because once we start, I am not going to want to stop."

"I want you. I really want you." Jessica stared right into his eyes as she spoke. "No stopping."

Griffin crushed her lips with a kiss then.

Chapter 16 - Saturday

E ventually, Jessica and Griffin climbed out of bed. Both of them grinning stupidly.

"We should shower," said Griffin.

"We should, but not together," grinned Jessica. "We'll never get going."

"You might be right." Griffin snatched a kiss from her. "Go shower and I'll make coffee. Then I'll shower and you make breakfast." He waggled his eyebrows at his offer.

Jessica laughed and agreed. It might not sound like an equal offer, but his coffees were delectable, and she didn't mind making breakfast.

In an hour they were clean, fed, and out the door, headed back to her old apartment to collect the rest of her stuff.

Then they managed to grocery shop, but neither felt like cooking by the time evening came around. "Can we just marinate the meat for tomorrow and order pizza?" suggested Jessica.

"That sounds like a damn good idea," agreed Griffin as he handed her a cider and dropped on the couch beside her. "Who needs a gym when you can move boxes and furniture all day?"

"Right?" chuckled Jessica. "Sorry. ...Do you go to a gym?"

"Do I look like I go to a gym?"

Jessica considered. He definitely had muscle, but he wasn't cut like he worked out often.

"Ummm,"

"Stop it. No, I obviously don't go to the gym. I do usually walk to work one or two days a week. And in the summer, I love being outdoors. But go to the gym? No."

"Hmm, me too. Well, no, I haven't been walking to work, but I would like to, now that it's within walking distance."

"Good, then we'll do that. But right now, I'm walking nowhere but within this house."

"Yup." Jesica tipped her head back and just relaxed. Griffin did the same. They were totally content to just sit for a little. Not asleep, but expending minimal energy.

Eventually though, afraid that she would stiffen up if she sat any longer, Jessica tossed her phone to Griffin and said, "You order pizza, I'll prep the food for tomorrow with Mellie."

"Yes, ma'am," said Griffin with mock solemnity.

Jessica made quick work of marinating the chicken and prepping the pasta salad. She had cheated heavily, buying coleslaw mix, so that would wait until tomorrow.

She no sooner finished than the doorbell rang and Griffin walked into the kitchen with two pizzas and two orders of wings.

"Wow dude! How hungry are you?" asked Jessica, looking at the four boxes.

"Don't you know cold pizza is perfect for breakfast?"

"Well, that is true."

"Right, so we need leftovers. And the two boxes of wings aren't really that much. We'll inhale those in no time."

"Ok, ok, you're right."

"I know." Griffin laughed as he spoke, and Jessica laughed right along with him.

"Maybe if I'm not having to cook breakfast tomorrow, maybe I'll make some protein bites and muffins for our work snacks."

"No wonder you were asking if I go to the gym. You're gonna make me fat!"

"Well, both of us then. But actually, they both have all sorts of healthy stuff and not that much fattening stuff."

"Uhhuh." Griffin didn't sound convinced. "We need to make sure your weekends aren't all about cooking for us. You need to spend time on your own writing, too. Your own creativity."

Jessica's face burned. No one had ever said something like that to her before.

"I don't mean to sound like a boss, but I don't want you so busy taking care of us that you lose you."

"Aww, Griff. You've grown up so much from that obnoxious teenager I last saw you as."

"I mean, I can find some frogs to stick in your bed, if you want."

Jessica snorted a laugh. "Um no, I'm good. Thanks." She bit her lip, "I mean it, though. You were kinda a jerk."

"Kinda?"

"Yeah, well, you were a huge jerk. But now you're not."

Griffin quirked his lips, "Thanks. Yeah, I dunno. Do boys just mature that much later? I had nothing in common with you then, you or Mellie. But I also wanted to be around you, cause you were obviously cooler than me."

"I don't think we were very cool. I was a book reading nerd then, too."

"You did always have a book with you. Notice I never ruined your books, though."

"Hmm, no," she chewed her lip. "You were a reader then, too. It was about the only thing we could talk about."

"Uhhuh, we didn't usually read too many of the same ones. We should do that."

"Huh?" Jessica was lost.

"We should each read the same book and chat about it as one of our date ideas."

"Ohhh," Jessica considered it. "Yeah, I'm game."

"Cool," Griffin grinned.

Yesterday, they had finished moving everything from Jessica's old apartment and returned the key. Plus, they had prepped food for today, so there was no reason to hurry out of bed. Unwilling to get out of bed, but unable to sleep longer, Jessica rolled over and grabbed her phone. Reflexively, she checked email and messenger for any texts, but then she pulled up the Kindle app. How glorious was it to have hundreds of books at her fingertips? An entire library of books she liked or wanted to try available at any time!

Eventually, the smell of coffee wafted up, and Jessica decided to crawl out of bed. Leggings, a t-shirt, and brushed teeth were about all she did to greet the world. She pulled her hair into a loose bun, because the ponytail didn't stay, as she came down the stairs.

"Ahhh, there you are. I thought maybe you had turned into a log, or jumped out the window and left me."

Jessica giggled at the outrageousness, and replied, "Nah, I was just being lazy and reading. But then this delectable scent wafted up."

"I think coffee is your love language."

"It's my 'be sociable language', that's for sure."

"Hmm," Griffin slid a freshly poured mug over to her. "Maybe that's it."

Jessica held the mug against her lips and just inhaled the magic scent for a moment before even taking a sip. The smell was just as good as the actual taste. Sometimes better, in fact.

The sun was shining through the window. One of those bright days that might be sunny and gorgeous, or maybe it carried false cheer and was sunny and frigid. Jessica pulled out her phone to take a look at the weather app. Her phone said 45.

"After I put on real clothes, wanna go for a walk and show off your neighborhood?"

Griffin lifted an eyebrow and looked out the window. "It looks nice, sure."

"My phone says it's already 45."

"Hells yes, then. Finish your coffee and wear what you have on. Let's tour the neighborhood. Maybe I can do a British accent and we can do our own version of the 'Homes of the Rich and Famous' or whatever that show was."

Jessica grinned, "Perfect, no bad British accent necessary, though." She pondered for a moment, "I think it was 'Lives of the Rich and Famous.'"

"Yup, that sounds more right. Whatever. You know what I meant." They both laughed.

Soon enough, they were out walking and chatting about whatever, just like they had the first afternoon, they were "stuck" together as they walked around Littleton. Being snowed in had been good for them, but Jessica preferred this warmer weather, and could hardly wait for summer.

"Isn't this one just like a gingerbread house?" asked Griffin, pointing across the street.

"Uhhuh, I expect Hansel and Gretel to come running out!" giggled Jessica. Then she pointed down the street, "But that one over there, how many shades of purple can one house have?!"

"Right? Hideous."

"Oh."

Jessica stopped short and Griffin knew exactly why. They had just come into sight of his favorite house. It looked just like a castle, with granite stonework behind a wrought-iron fence. Behind it was the ocean, and because of this, the salt air had caused a rusty patina on the crevices of the wrought iron, making it look like dark walnut from a distance. But it was the two towers on the corners of the house that really gave it personality, with a long balcony stretching between them and the house behind. It was a gorgeous house.

"You wanna know the best part?"

"Huh? What?" asked Jessica, tearing her eyes off the castle.

"They do teas and lawn parties in the summer. So once it warms up to summer temperatures, we can tour the grounds and some of the house, including one of those towers and the balcony. There are matching towers and balconies on the back side overlooking the ocean, too. We can also climb up those."

"Really?" asked Jessica with excitement.

"Uhhuh. And they are pretty friendly to artists. They often allow a painter on their grounds, one side or the other. I bet they would let you sit there and write if the ambiance helped you."

"That would be super cool." Jessica grinned at the thought. "Talk about slipping into the scene."

"Right." Griffin couldn't help but smile at her happiness. He thought the castle was cool, but it was just something to look at. It seemed to breathe energy into Jessica. And that made him happy.

Jessica and Mellie had a blast looking through old pictures that Jessica unpacked just for this. They kept showing photos to Griffin, and he teased them for their haircuts and their clothes. Sometimes just for the goofy facial expressions. Finally, Mellie vowed to bring pictures of him next week when she came over.

They spent the afternoon talking about growing up. When they were younger, they had played together. High school gave them different circles of friends, but the same activities of Spirit Week, cafeteria goop and cheese, assemblies, sports coaches, etc.

"Ok, Lovebirds, I need to get home," said Mellie finally.

Jessica blushed, but Griffin just grinned. "Fine, Sis."

Mellie and Jessica walked to the car and giggled a little. Griffin pretended not to hear them as it seemed that his sis had his back and it could only benefit him.

He did pause a moment while washing their glasses, considering that they might be planning on how to get back at him for all the pranks he had played on them in the past. *Would she be that conniving?*

After Mellie had left, they did some more work to be ready for the week, washing laundry, checking online payments, and snack prepping. It was boring, but comfortable. Griffin was smiling at the surprise he had arranged for Jessica at the office, but she missed it because she was creating her last freelance invoice.

Finally, they settled into just relaxing.

"So, what book should we read together?" asked Griffin.

"Right, I forgot about that." She chewed her lip for a moment. "What type of books do you like?"

"I'm pretty open to try anything reasonable," Griffin started.

"Reasonable?" she interrupted.

"Well, I'm not sure I'm ready for tentacle porn."

"No tentacle porn, got it." Jessica was grinning.

"Yeah, so I don't think I've ever read romance at all, but lots of thrillers, horror, nonfiction, I don't know."

"Hmm, I read all those," seeing Griffin about to interrupt, "Ok, not *all* of those, no tentacle porn or alien porn, but the other genres. I read a lot of fantasy, too."

"Like *Lord of the Rings*?"

"More like *Game of Thrones* and ACOTAR."

"ACOTAR?"

"Yeah, it's an acronym, but it's fantasy romance, so probably not your thing."

"Ah." Griffin contemplated and spoke slowly, "*Lord of the Rings* was mostly slow, like I liked *The Hobbit*, but not the rest. *Game of Thrones* was a great show. Except for the ending."

"Yeah well, HBO didn't have a good script to work from for the ending. George RR Martin hadn't finished the series yet. Not their fault."

"Maybe we could find something by Sanderson we would like. He writes fantasy and has intricate worlds. Usually the storylines are fairly complicated."

"Are they standalones or series?"

"Good point, mostly series."

"Ok, let's look for a couple of standalones first. A fantasy, a murder mystery, and something historical fiction or biographical."

"Yeah, I'm down with that. Then we'll choose." Jessica nodded, smiling. "Do we care what format?"

"Format?"

"Audio, kindle, print?'

"Oh. I don't care."

"Ok."

They fell down a rabbit hole of searching through book titles and blurbs. Not following the plan, they each suggested multiple books to each other, including some that sounded horrible. While perusing, Griffin choked on his beer. After gulping in some air, he said, "Clearly our devices are listening. Here's an ad for *My Alien's Third Arm*."

"Um, not that one, please. I don't even want the blurb." Jessica giggled.

"Imagine what I could do with a third arm?" Griffin waggled his eyebrows suggestively.

"Or me," snorted Jessica.

"Fair point." They both laughed.

"We need more wine for this."

"We should read it just to see how bad it is."

"No. No, we shouldn't."

He clicked 'buy now'.

Chapter 17 - Monday

The next morning as they were getting ready for work, Griffin poured coffee for Jessica and said, "Listen, on Tuesdays I usually hang out with some buddies and bowl or play softball or something. You're welcome to join if you want."

"How come you didn't go last week?"

"Well, ya know, it was your first couple of days here."

"You silly," Jessica couldn't help but smile though. He was so sweet. "Yeah, no. You head out and have a blast with your friends. I don't need a babysitter. I actually enjoy alone time."

Griffin stared at her. "Are you sure?"

"Yeah, I used to live alone. I like quiet time, too."

"OK, well, if you change your mind, you're welcome. This week or any other."

"Noted. Thank you. I might listen to an audiobook, we'll see."

"Ok. Ready?"

"Yup, let me grab my bag."

Apparently Mondays were for setting a plan for the week, and looking ahead for challenges and successes, Tuesdays were for a general staff meeting to see if a department needed anything or how they could best support each other, tossing out ideas, and generally a fair amount of laughing with brainstorming. Or so Jessica had been told. Sitting at her desk Monday morning, she had no idea what to bring to Tuesday's meeting.

Just then, there was a soft knock on her open door. "Have a minute?" asked Mike with a smile.

"Hey, yeah. Absolutely," said Jessica, pushing her laptop to the side.

"Whatchya workin' on?" asked Mike, as he lounged on the little sofa.

"Honestly, I was thinking about tomorrow's meeting. What the heck am I supposed to bring to the table?"

"Good, that's why I stopped by." Mike grinned at her. "Tomorrow is not a day that I expect you to report out on anything or come with a slew of ideas of how to work with all the departments. Tomorrow, I figure you'll do a lot of learning about our personalities and our talents. I would like you to bring a few examples of work that you have done so you can show everyone, but they'll understand that what you have been doing isn't exactly what we do, so it's not gonna be a great match, but you can show off what you can do." He blinked quickly a moment. "Did that even make sense?"

"Ok, so like a mini portfolio of 'I can't wait to work with you, here's some stuff I've done, let's talk about what you need?'"

"Exactly!" Mike's smile returned. "And, we have some avid readers on staff so you could mention that you are also an indie-author. You might get them to buy some books."

"Oh my god, yeah maybe not yet."

"Self-conscious?"

"Wicked. Like professional stuff can be judged all you want, but my stories, oof. That's terrifying."

"I don't think you need to be. But ok, let that just come up in conversation if you want."

Jessica let out a breath and purposely relaxed her shoulders. "Ok."

"We had some cool ideas when we were talking. You and I, during your interview, bring up some of those if you want tomorrow. Or take tomorrow to get to know us better. Our brainstorming sessions get a little loud and silly sometimes, but it seems to be how we work. I hear that people like you, so just be you."

"Yeah?" she bit her lip, suddenly nervous again.

"Yeah. I got your back. And if I didn't, I bet Griffin would."

"Probably."

"Ok, let me know if you have questions. You can always pop into my office or shoot me an email." When Jessica nodded, he added, "Right, I'm going downstairs to grab a coffee. Want anything?"

"No thanks," Jessica said it cheerily, but it blew her away. She had never had a boss offer to get her coffee or a snack before. At this rate she would be a fat, hyper-caffeinated little worker bunny between him, Griffin, and the occasional other people who offered. Jessica wasn't used to just heading to the local coffee shop when she wanted coffee. She had been too cheap for years. But she pondered that maybe she should make a tray of cookies to bring in for everyone being so nice to her. There was a staff room with a fridge, etc. She could just leave them on the table.

Jessica: Hey is there molasses at the house?

Griffin: Ummm. I have no idea why?

Jessica: I was thinking about making cookies. I'll need ground ginger and molasses.

Griffin: That doesn't go bad, does it? We'll just stop and buy some.

Jessica: k, thanks.

Another knock on her office door frame startled Jessica from the promo image she was creating as a mockup. Graphic design always had her second guessing herself. She blew a strand of hair out of her face and called "Come in!" while looking up.

To her surprise, Kara, from the Front Desk was standing there with an enormous basket and flowers. "You," she said with a grin, "have a delivery!"

"What?" asked Jessica, taken completely aback.

"Here, we'll place these gorgeous flowers on this table by your window so you can see them all day, but they're not in the way." She placed the happy-looking tulips on the table and plucked out the card. "And these we'll set here within easy reach." Onto the corner of Jessica's desk, she placed the card from the flowers and the basket filled with chocolate muffins, wrapped with a red bow. "We are all officially jealous, just so you know."

"Oh my! I have never received anything like this." Jessica could feel the heat in her cheeks. She had a very good idea of who had sent these. "Here, grab a muffin. I don't need them all, and they look yummy."

"I bet whoever sent these is yummy, too." Kara winked, grabbed a muffin and headed back out of the office.

Jessica grinned and leaned back in her chair, stretching out her neck. She bet Griffin was right across the hall, waiting to hear her reaction. They usually kept their doors open, and she was sure he was almost wiggling in anticipation. She leaned forward to grab the little envelope and slid her thumbnail under the corner. She was a tangled mess of excited and nervous to read it. With another guy, she might have worried that this was a 'thanks for the sex we're through now' kind of thing, but he hadn't acted that way at all. So what was this?

She slid the card out,

Hope you like them even though they can't possibly be as pretty or sweet as you.

Take all the time you need. Dinner date tonight?

Oh, he was sweet! They had been cuddly and playful all weekend, but each was in their own bed at night. He wasn't rushing her at all, even though they had already slept together. He might really be a keeper.

She stood up and slipped across the hall. Surely the gossips would figure out he had sent her the basket and flowers. They arrived and left nearly every day together, but no reason to add to the gossip fodder.

Griffin looked up with a grin as she slipped in and raised his eyebrows when she closed his door.

"Thank you," she said and tossed him a muffin.

"For what?" he asked coyly.

"For what. For the very pretty flowers and the basket of chocolate yumminess. And...thank you."

"Yeah," he smiled gently. "I mean it. Take all the time you need. Although I do like the friends with benefits thing while we ...date." He grinned and waggled his eyebrows overly suggestively at the end.

Jessica laughed too. "Yeah, that's fun."

"Mhhmm. So dinner out tonight?"

"Oh, I forgot that part. Umm, sure."

"Cool, I'll pick you up at like 6, ok? You live awfully close to me."

"You're an idiot," laughed Jessica. Turning back as she opened the office door, "Sure. 6 is fine."

Jessica kept grinning all morning while she worked and nibbled on two muffins. They ought not to go stale, she reasoned. She would have to decide whether to bring them home this afternoon or keep them in her office. The entire room smelled fresh and chocolaty now.

Graphic designing went better with snacks too, and she soon had about ten mock-ups created to bring to tomorrow's meeting.

Jessica was feeling good. It was an agreeable change to her life. No longer just living, but really enjoying life.

Chapter 18 - Day to Day

Soon Jessica and Griffin had a great routine. At least once a week, they would go out on a date. They would each dress up a little and then go to dinner, or bowling, or whatever. They would laugh and laugh, but they did that all the time, anyway. If they didn't stay out too late, they would curl up on the couch together and watch tv or work on some projects.

One evening it was freezing rain, so they decided to postpone their date night. They picked up sushi and other snacks from the grocery store and hung out in the living room together. They put on a tv series and just watched episode after episode while snacking and chatting. It was the most low key date ever.

"Why do we need a label?" asked Griffin. "This works for me."

"You don't want more?" asked Jessica.

"I mean...I'm not opposed to more. But I don't *need* more."

"What about when people ask you if you're seeing someone?"

"Oh, you know me, I can deflect."

"But I don't want you to deflect. Or," Jessica took a breath, "I don't want you to have to deflect."

"Ok."

"I don't want to hide us together."

"Oh, I don't think we're hidden. Anyone seeing us together probably knows."

Jessica laughed, 'Yeah, you're right."

Griffin chuckled too, then said, "I don't need us to have a label. We can be friends, we can be friends with benefits, we can be dating, we can be roommates... whatever you want."

"Stupid labels," said Jessica in mock anger. "I think it's pretty apparent we're dating. We'll go with that."

"Ok. Your call. But only if they ask."

"You don't want to claim me on your social media accounts."

"I mean, um-"

"Relax," laughed Jessica. "I don't care."

Griffin's phone chimed, and a second later, so did Jessica's.

"Well, it's either really good or really bad," said Griffin.

Jessica scooped up her phone from the couch beside her once she located it under a throw pillow. A group chat from Mellie was the cause.

Hey lovebirds! Fancy another trip to VT? Someone needs to head up for a few days so the furnace guys can do some more work.

Jessica raised her eyebrows as she read and felt herself blush. She didn't even know why, really. "Well now," she said.

"Hmm, whaddya think?" Griffin thought it sounded great, but waited to see what Jessica thought before responding.

"I mean, we didn't really get to ski last time between them leaving early and then the ice storm. That could be fun, and it's nearly the end of the season now."

"Sure, and we can both work remotely if we want to. Or we could just take it off."

"Yeah, see, I'm kinda fond of eating, so I want my paycheck." Jessica twisted her hair around a finger while she thought. "We could take off one day, though, to ski and whatever."

"Whatever?" Griffin flirted.

"Shut up!" Jessica laughed and hit him with a pillow.

"Well, you said it," grinned Griffin.

"Uhhuh." Jessica replied to the chat. *Yeah, we can go. When?*

Griffin added, *Preferably not tomorrow, we have freezing rain tonight.*

Yeah, Mellie replied, *here too. Next week?*

Sure.

Ok.

Ok, I'll have mom set it up and call you with the details. Mellie was happy to pass this chore off and she thought they might enjoy the trip.

"Hmm, a cabin in the woods with a pretty girl." Griffin made it sound like a Hallmark movie.

"Oh, shut up." Jessica couldn't help but laugh with Griffin, though. That snowy cabin was where they had reconnected and started this, whatever this was.

"Ok seriously, though. We'll be able to work up there a day or two and we can take a day or two off. Plus the weekend, we could spend a whole week up there. We can ski a day or two depending on the weather and on the not so nice days, work inside."

"Yeah, I mean, it totally doesn't sound horrible. I'm not sure where my skis are. I think they're buried in your shed out back."

"Ugh, yeah probably. But that's fine. Mine are too."

Ok, then I want to focus and get this project done so Mike can look at it tomorrow and give me feedback. Sometimes it's easier when we're standing next to each other looking, than asynchronously.

"Fine," said Griffin with mock disappointment. "I'll just have to eat this all alone while you slave away to your work."

"Umm, no. I'm pretty sure I can eat and work simultaneously."

"Oh, yeah?"

"Yeah."

"Hmm. I know what will help, too." So saying, Griffin hopped up and went to the fridge for a cold cider for Jessica and a beer for himself.

"Ahh, perfect," said Jessica, clinking the neck of her bottle against Griffin's. "Thank you."

Jessica and Griffin arrived at the cabin in Vermont late on Monday night. They worked a full day on a large project that the whole team was on, then drove a few hours to the Northeast Kingdom. They would be there for the rest of the week. The furnace guys were supposed to come the next day, Tuesday, and take a day or two. So Jessica and Griffin would work remotely on Tuesday and maybe Wednesday. Then they would check the weather to see what they wanted to do Thursday - Sunday. They wanted to ski, and they wanted to relax, and they could work when they felt like it.

"Brrr, doesn't feel like the furnace is hardly working. It's got to be like 40 in here." Jessica shivered. She dropped her bags and went over to check the thermostat.

"Yeah, Mellie said it keeps running at all sorts of temperatures - either way too high or way too low."

"Yeah, well, we're on a too low right now. It's 45. I was close."

"Awesome, or should I say, 'cool'?" Griffin laughed darkly. "Ok, can you get the woodstove started and I'll bring in more wood? We have those McD's wrappers and a paper bag if there isn't any paper to start it."

"I should be able to get it going. But see, stopping for a snack was a good idea."

"Right," Griffin called over his shoulder as he headed out for an armload of wood.

Jessica had grown up with woodstoves, so she had no problem shoveling out some cold ashes, then laying down paper and kindling. There were only two medium pieces of wood so she hoped Griffin brought in a couple more of those. The fire would start easier with smaller pieces and then they could feed it big ones to carry through the night. She was hunting for a lighter or matches as he came in through the door, stomping the dirt and snow off his boots before walking gingerly across the floor.

"Don't worry about your boots. I'll sweep it up."

"Thanks. Did you get it started?"

"No, I'm looking for a lighter." Just then, Jessica saw it tucked against the side of the cupboard next to some birthday candles. "Found it! Hey did you grab any smallish pieces? There isn't much in here between kindling and full pieces."

"Umm, no, I don't think I did, but I can grab some on this next load. I was going to grab one more load, anyway."

"Thanks!" Jessica held the door open for him and then, using the lighter, coaxed flames from the paper to lick the kindling.

Griffin stomped in through the door a moment later and dropped the armload of wood into the woodbox. He handed Jessica two smaller pieces of wood. "Here."

"Perfect, thank you." Jessica carefully positioned the two new pieces diagonally over the other pieces and then set a larger piece on top. She mostly closed the stove's door, creating a perfect draft. They could hear the fire eating hungrily, and the air whistling through as the draft caught. Soon heat began to come from the stove.

"It's gonna take a little while to warm it up in here. Want something warm to drink while it does?" Jessica asked Griffin as she grabbed the broom and dustpan.

"Yeah, that would be good." He pulled off his boots and sighed, wiggling his toes. "I'll bring our bags up. Do you want your computer left down here?"

"Umm, yeah. Thanks." Jessica scooped the muddy snow up and deposited it into the trash. There was so little it would evaporate before long. Then she filled the teakettle and turned it on. She pulled out mugs and the chai tea they both enjoyed. She rummaged through the cooler to pull out the cream and put cold foods into the fridge. They hadn't brought a lot, but enough for tonight's snacks and tomorrow's meals. Then they would have to grab some groceries.

Griffin came down the stairs biting a smile back, but didn't say anything. He had put all the bags up in his room. It was larger after all. He was hoping Jessica would be ok with it.

He sat down at the counter and plugged his cell phone in. *We made it;* he sent to the group chat. *It's a bit chilly in here, but Jessica got the wood stove going, so it'll be fine.*

A moment later their phones chimed with Melli's reply, *Cold enough for pipes to freeze?*

Nah, replied Griffin. "What did you say the temperature was?"

"45" answered Jessica as she poured their tea. Then she slid the containers with muffins and cookies over.

45 is chilly but not freezing. We'll talk to you tomorrow.

K, g'night.

Jessica poured a dollop of cream into her tea. Then she leaned against the counter, contentedly munching a chocolate chip cookie. The only sounds for the next few minutes were the sounds of the fire eating the kindling and then the shift of the logs in the stove.

"Sounds like it's caught well," commented Griffin.

"Yup, I think so," agreed Jessica. She grabbed another cookie and her mug of tea and moved over to the couch. She draped a throw blanket over her legs.

Griffin followed her over to the couch. "Let me cuddle up to you so we can share warmth." He grinned innocently.

Jessica laughed and lifted the blanket to share. "I suppose it's even colder upstairs?"

"Well, it's about the same, but it will warm up faster down here, closer to the stove. I turned on the fan in the stairwell, but it'll take a while."

"Yeah." Jessica bit her lip. "I suppose once we're under covers we'll warm up pretty fast, but I hate to be cold."

"I can warm you up." Griffin waggled his eyebrows as he suggested it, and then blinked innocently.

"Rouge," laughed Jessica.

"Ok, or we could grab sleeping bags and sleep down here by the stove."

"Hmm, that's a possibility, too." She chewed another bite of cookie while she considered. "So uncomfortable floor and warmer or colder and softer."

"Yup, pretty much," agreed Griffin.

"Hmm."

"I think bed, but I'll do what you want," said Griffin.

"You don't need to suffer through my choice," replied Jessica.

"No, but I like you and misery loves company."

Jessica laughed. "I don't think we'll be miserable, just not as comfortable."

"True. I might have exaggerated."

"Ok, I choose bed. I'm tired." Jessica put her mug in the sink. Griffin loaded the stove full of wood, so Jessica grabbed his mug and brought it to the sink, too.

"After you," said Griffin as he swept his arm towards the stairs. His voice stayed light, but he was nervous about whether Jessica would want to stay in his room.

Chapter 19 - Tuesday

Jessica blinked as the morning sunlight hit her eyes. She stretched, careful not to wake Griffin. His breathing was still deep and even beside her.

Last night, she had been a little shocked by his risk of assuming she would sleep with him without offering a choice like he always did. It wasn't that he forced her by any means, but he usually let her take the lead, always mindful of her comfort level. Her ex had done a whole mind-fuck on her and he respected her for learning to trust again.

But last night, she hesitated only a moment before agreeing to share a bed with him. It was COLD upstairs. They took turns in the bathroom and then slipped into the bed together. While she had been brushing her teeth Griffin had stripped the blankets from the spare room. She wore a t-shirt and gym shorts; he wore pajama bottoms and they spooned for a while until the bed warmed up. By morning, they had rolled apart, but he had a hand on her arm and she had a leg against his. Jessica smiled. She was sure no one would believe that they literally just slept together, not even any kissing with the cuddles, but this was just one more example of him being sweet.

Jessica slipped out of bed, for once successfully getting up without waking him. Maybe it had taken him a long time to fall asleep, but she had quickly (unusually) fallen asleep and slept soundly all night long. Jessica stealthily grabbed her bag and tiptoed to her room to get dressed. She left all the doors open so the heat could freely move through the cabin.

Once downstairs, she stirred the stove to life, unburying the live coals and gently laying some mid-sized, very dry wood on it. She left the stove door cracked open for the draft and got the coffee pot ready.

After checking the stove and adding more wood, she scribbled a quick note and left it by the coffeepot.

Just hit the on switch, coffee is ready to go. I went for a quick walk since there's no gym, be back soon.

The morning was crisp and cold, but the sun was glittering off of every surface. The temperature was still below freezing but the sun itself was shining down warmth and the icicles were just starting to melt with water drops barely clinging to the tips.

It was far from quiet though as she crunched up the side of the road. Birds were calling, especially the chickadees chattering. True to her word, Jessica was back in about half an hour. She opened the door to the scent of coffee and she grinned.

"Hey you," said Griffin. "I made the coffee, so you're making breakfast."

Jessica snorted. "You flicked the switch, huh?"

"Sure did. Here's the cream." Griffin set the cream on the counter.

"Ok," said Jessica with a grin, "I'll make an equally difficult breakfast. Toast will be ready in five."

"Touche," laughed Griffin.

"Right." Jessica poured her coffee, added cream, and stared at him, leaning against the counter, holding the mug at her lips and inhaling the wonderful scent.

Griffin grinned. "So we have that quiche already made, right? I was about to take that out. Or we could do something else."

"No, that sounds good. It'll take like twenty minutes to reheat in the oven, or you can slice it and microwave it, but the crust won't be crispy."

"I'm not starving. What temp?" Griffin outstretched his hand to the buttons on the stove.

"I don't know," Jessica considered. "350? 400?"

"375, got it."

Jessica laughed and pulled the tinfoil covered glass pie plate out of the fridge. She handed it to Griffin, and he slid it into the oven.

"Ok then, I'm going to take a quick shower. Don't wait for me when it's ready." Saying that, Griffin bounced up the stairs.

"Right." Jessica considered her options and decided to do ten minutes of yoga and then claim a space to set up her laptop to work. Today, they were working remotely while the furnace crew was there. She wanted to sit at the table by the window, but decided the glare would be a problem all day. Instead, she set up at the bar counter of the kitchen. She plugged in her computer even though it was half charged and grabbed her notebook and multi colored pens. She had been laughed at a lot over the multi-color inks in her planner, but she always knew what was upcoming and what was due, in person, online, for work, personal, and her writing. It was a simple system and easy to understand at a glance.

The oven beeped that it had reached temperature as Jessica refilled her coffee, adding a few drops of chocolate syrup this time. Maybe a fancy mocha would get her into work mode, because she wasn't feeling it. Then she took the grapes from the cooler and dumped them into a colander to rinse off. Good brain food for the workday and better for her hips than the chocolate chip cookies that were calling her name. She could smell the quiche then, so she carefully lifted the tinfoil off for the last few minutes of baking.

"Perfect timing?" asked Griffin as he bounced down the stairs, still toweling off his hair.

"Almost. It needs a minute or two," said Jessica as she flipped the oven to broil.

"Good, I'm ravenous." Looking around then he raised his eyebrows. "Really? You don't want to work from the couch?"

"Nah, I'm not feeling it right now. But you know me. I'll probably move to the floor later."

He chuckled, "You always do. I think the girls at work are nearly used to it now."

The first time Mike had seen her working on the floor, papers spread all around her, he lifted an eyebrow but didn't say anything else. The next day, there were two large floor pillows and a lap desk waiting for her.

Jessica was pulling the quiche out just as there was a knock at the door. Griffin let in the furnace guys and offered them coffee as Jessica cut the quiche.

"Should I offer that to them, too?" whispered Griffin. "It was supposed to be breakfast for us twice."

"Just offer it," Jessica whispered back. And, sure enough, the workers said no, although they might appreciate coffee later.

"No problem," said Jessica. "The pot will be on all day. I like my coffee."

"She really does," laughed Griffin as he sat down beside her to eat.

About 4:30 that afternoon, the furnace guys called it a day, saying they thought they would be done in under two hours the next day, but they would have to wait for a part. Hopefully, it would be delivered to the warehouse first thing.

Jessica had finished her work about an hour before and was doing some of her own writing. Griffin decided that everyone else being done was a sign, and he shut his computer down.

"Let's get out of here," he said.

"Ok, where?"

"I hear there's a little brewery in East Haven, like ten minutes from here. Let's try it."

"Enh, micro beer isn't really my thing."

"If they don't have any good microbrews or carry anything you like, then we'll just keep going and hit The Tavern in Island Pond."

"The Tavern? I thought it was The Essex House?"

"Whatever it's called," Griffin agreed.

"Yeah, ok. Give me five minutes to get ready."

"Kk."

Since the furnace was completely non-functioning right now, Griffin loaded up the stove, unsure of how long they would be gone. They really had no timeframe, but he wanted the cabin still warm when they got back.. They apparently wouldn't be skiing tomorrow either, since the furnace guys would be back once they got their part, and who knew when that would be? He wasn't upset, but he was a little cranky about it. He had hoped to ski. He felt a little better when he checked the forecast and saw it was supposed to be a gloomy, cloudy day tomorrow. Better to ski on a sunny, fun day. He flopped down on the couch with the book he was sort of reading.

Jessica came down the stairs a couple of minutes later. She looked perplexed.

"Hey, listen to this," she said.

"Yeah?" asked Griffin, sitting up.

"This doesn't seem like spam, but it's odd." She handed her phone over to Griffin with an email open on the screen.

As he started reading it, he mumbled, "Oh, no shit. You got in!" He looked up at her and grinned.

"Wait, what? Got into what?"

"Well," Griffin gave his best golden retriever grin. "I might have signed you up for this. I um...I didn't tell you in case you didn't get in."

"You what?" asked Jessica with a nervous laugh.

Griffin stood up and handed her phone back. "It's legit. And, you're an amazing cook, so I, um, I signed you up for a cooking competition."

"What?!"

"You're an amazing cook, so I signed you up for a competition and they accepted you."

"They accepted me without tasting any of my food??"

"Yup." Griffin scratched his chin. "They might have seen some photos."

"What?" Jessica was too stressed to worry that she sounded like a broken record.

"Yeah, it'll be fine. C'mon. Let's get a drink and we'll talk about it on the way."

In a daze, Jessica pulled on her boots and coat. Griffin had remotely started the car, so it was already warmish inside.

Griffin headed down to the main road and then north towards East Haven. "So the Dirt Church Brewery is actually right on the town line of East Haven and Newark," said Griffin.

"Newark? There's a Newark here? Like New Jersey?"

"Probably not quite like New Jersey," Griffin chuckled. "Yeah, apparently it's another one of these small towns. But I don't know anything about it. Vermont has a ton of small towns that you don't even know exist unless you see it on a map."

"Yeah," Jessica laughed back. "Ok, you just hit me with two new things here, one a little bigger than the other. So tell me about where we're going first. Is it like a huge brewery or like they brew one thing at a time and we all drink it?"

"Umm, I don't know much about it. I know they took an old church and remodeled it. I think they serve local brews and their own."

"Ok, so cute and cozy, with at least a little variety. Do they have cider?"

"Yeah, so," Griffin grimaced. "That's one thing I didn't see on the menu. But they have beer, of course, wine and a local seltzer."

"Ok. We'll try it. And they must have snacks, too."

"Yeah."

Griffin let her ride in silence for a couple of minutes. Then he asked, "Ok, what are you thinking?"

"I'm thinking about all the Ramsey cooking shows that I have watched." Jessica gave a little depreciating laugh.

"This won't be like that," chuckled Griffin. "This is held at a hotel in Mass. They take over the whole place and set up a bunch of cooking stations. Then, umm, have you ever seen the show, *Chopped*? The one where they get a basket of ingredients for each round?"

"Yeah? Is that what this is?" Jessica was beginning to panic.

"Half of it. There are two rounds for each part of the meal. One round you get a basket, one round you get to choose your own."

"Huh," Jessica pushed down the panic and actually thought about it. That was a cool design for a cooking competition. "And someone gets eliminated on each round?"

"Yeah," Griffin pulled the word out as if he were unsure. "I think so, but I don't really know."

"Ok."

"Are there attachments to the email?"

"Yeah, but I don't have enough service to open them right now." Jessica checked her phone again, but still only one bar.

"Ha, small town life. Maybe there will be Wi-Fi at the bar."

"We must be almost there," said Jessica, looking at the map app on her phone. Luckily, she had started it as they left the cabin and had service.

"Yeah, here's the main part of East Haven," agreed Griffin.

"Where?" asked Jessica, a little bewildered.

"Well, the town garage with the road sand and salt is up here on the left, but the school and 'main streets,'" he air quoted that, "are on your right."

"Really?"

"Yeah."

"Umm,"

"I know. It looks like all the rest of the road. A logger here and a home hairstylist, but yeah, the center of town."

"Wait, isn't East Haven the old army base?"

"What?"

"Yeah, I swear I read that somewhere. They built a radar tower up on one of these mountains and the base, the housing and whatnot, down at the bottom. I think that was East Haven."

"Well, I guess that might explain why it's so tight and all on that one side of the road, but I don't know."

"Oh!" Jessica was brought out of her thoughts when she saw Dirt Church pop up on her map app. "It's just up on the left. The bar, I mean."

"Probably that open flag, huh?"

"Oh, and there's the church just past it," added Jessica.

"Huh, I thought it was in the church."

"Yeah." Jessica pulled her hair back in a new ponytail as they pulled into the little parking lot. "There's a few cars, at least. But it looks tiny."

"Yeah. We'll try it, but we don't have to stay."

"Uhhuh." Jessica grinned. "It might be cool."

"Hey folks!" a chipper bartender greeted them. "I need to run downstairs to change out a keg, and then I'll be right back, ok?" He gave them a bright smile and waited for them to reply before hurrying to the corner and apparently the stairs.

"Yeah, no worries. We need to read what you have," said Griffin.

Jessica and Griffin sat at the end of the bar, where there were three high-backed stools. They climbed up and perused the board. There were names like Trail Angel and Church Key. Each one listed whether it was a pale ale or lager or wine, as well as the alcohol content.

"I think I'm going with the seltzer," said Jessica.

"Yeah? I think I'll do the Grade A Fancy," replied Griffin.

The bartender was just coming back around the counter. "Grade A?" he repeated. "And yours?" he asked Jessica. "Sorry, I didn't hear what you said."

"I think I'll try the seltzer."

"Sure, of course. Which one?" He moved back and pointed to two different signs.

"What kind of question is that, Darren? Give her the house one," said a woman with long, blond hair standing at the other end of the L-shaped bar.

Darren grinned. "This one here is what we make on this site. And this one," he pointed at the other sign, "is canned in Lyndonville. It's a little sweeter, I'm told, and there are a couple flavors."

"Hmm," Jessica bit her lip while she thought.

So Darren poured a Grade A Fancy for Griffin. "Decide yet?" he asked Jessica with a smile. Do you want a sample of Bright and Tight? The house one?"

"Yeah, can you do that?"

"Sure. Of course!"

He took a shot glass and filled it with seltzer from a tap.

Jessica blinked in surprise, but really liked it when she tasted it. "Yeah, I'll have a glass of that, please."

Darren grinned again. "Yeah, you liked it? Perfect, coming right up."

"And you have some food?" asked Griffin.

"Um, well yeah. A little." Darren handed over a glass filled to the rim with seltzer. "We have some pizzas, pretzels with mustard, and this popcorn here. I haven't started the oven yet, but I can do that now. A pizza would be like 20 minutes."

"Sometimes we have the food truck here," chimed in the blond again.

"Yeah, I think they're here for lunch this weekend, right?" Darren replied back to her.

"Yeah, one of the days. I don't remember if it's Saturday or Sunday, though."

"I'll have to look on the schedule," said Darren. He ducked into the back room, and the blond followed him.

Griffin and Jessica looked at each other and just laughed. "I take it she works here too," chuckled Griffin.

"Yeah." Jessica kept smiling, "So um, I'm not really feeling frozen pizza."

"Yeah, no. I'm munchy, but none of that is calling me."

"No,"

"Except maybe the food truck, but that doesn't help us now."

"Nah," agreed Jessica. "How's that Fancy A, Grade A, whatever you have?"

"Grade A Fancy. I like it. How's yours?"

"Yeah, it's good. Fruity, but not in your face sweet. I could probably drink a lot of these."

"I bet they have some you can buy. See, they have a cooler of cans there."

"Oh, yeah." Jessica looked over at the cooler and the counter beside it. There was also a huge glass jar with dog cookies, salt and pepper shakers, napkins, and some pamphlets of local attractions.

Looking around more, Jessica liked the decor. This building was not the church, but it had a little sitting area in one corner with a couple of church pews set up with pillows and an acoustic guitar. The walls were wood, actually everything was wood finished and with wooden beams. On the walls were signs from the local ski and bike trails. There were also other outdoorsy decorations.

Griffin leaned over to Jessica when he came back from the restroom. "You should check that out."

"Check what out?" she asked, confused.

"The bathroom," Griffin laughed. "The walls are covered in ski area/biking trail maps and then there's a ton of stickers from different resorts and businesses, too."

"Like wall paper?" asked Jessica, trying to picture it.

"Yeah, you'll see. It's cool though."

"Ok, I'll look later."

Darren came back to them. "Need another?" he asked them both.

"Not yet," said Jessica. "It's good though."

"Yeah, you like it? Good." Darren grinned at her. "What about you? Ready for another?" he asked Griffin.

Griffin looked at Jessica and raised his eyebrows with a silent question.

"Yeah, we'll stay for a while," she said.

"Ok, then, I'll take another," said Griffin, sliding his empty glass forward.

Darren made quick work of rinsing the glass and refilling it. Then he went to serve someone else next to the blond woman at the other end of the bar.

"Ok, tell me more about this contest you entered me in."

Griffin laughed softly. "Hopefully, you're not mad."

"I don't know whether to be mad yet," replied Jessica with a grimace.

"Yeah, so about it. Let's see. It's on a weekend, a Saturday, I think. It's kinda an all day thing. You don't have to bring any tools or supplies, you use just what they furnish. You might be able to bring recipes with you, but I'm not sure. But I don't think you use recipes, anyway."

"I use recipes," Jessica protested.

"Not ones written down," countered Griffin.

"Well, no. Not usually," agreed Jessica.

"Uhhuh. Like I said, there are three courses you do, just like *Chopped*, with an appetizer, and entrée and a dessert. And it's like *Chopped*, where they give you a basket of ingredients for each of those and a time limit."

"And a round for each where I can make anything I want."

"Yup."

"Uhhuh. How much did it cost?"

"Not much," Griffin hedged.

"How much?"

"I think it was $10. It was definitely less than $20. I think it covers the cost of your apron, 'cause you get to keep that."

"Uhhuh. How much time is each round?"

"I don't know. Probably not long," chuckled Griffin.

"It probably says in the email, but I still don't have service." Jessica finished her drink. She was a mixture of irritation and excited about the idea of a cooking contest.

"Want another?" asked Griffin, looking at her empty glass.

"Yeah, I'll be right back. I need to check out this amazing bathroom."

Griffin laughed. "Ok."

She narrowed her eyes at him, a new thought concerning her.

"What?" he asked.

"How many people did you tell about this?"

"No one." Griffin held up his hands in mock surrender.

"Not even Mellie?"

"I didn't tell anyone, I swear."

"Uhhuh." Jessica paused and then added, "I don't know whether to believe you or not. I don't know whether to hate you or be excited. I never would have signed up for this."

"I know. But I think you could win."

"And if I don't?"

"So what? Besides, you get a new apron."

"I don't wear aprons."

"Well..."

"Get me a drink." Jessica rolled her eyes and slipped off the stool. It could be fun, she considered. It would also be stressful. She didn't think she could win, but she might make it at least halfway. *Can you even practice for such a thing?*

Chapter 20 - Thursday and Friday

Wednesday was a very slow and uneventful day. Jessica hit the grocery store while Griffin stayed at the cabin for the furnace guys. He could have come though, because they didn't receive the part until after lunch.

Meanwhile, in the late morning, Jessica baked muffins and made some energy balls for ski snacks the next day. Then they both put in a full day's worth of remote work. That evening, Griffin took a turn doing dinner with grilled steaks ("The grill still works in winter, your hands just get cold," he said), baked potato, salad, and wine.

By evening, they were both a little stir crazy and chatting excitedly about skiing the next day. They were both strong skiers, though neither was racing material. They were comfortable to go on any trail on the mountain.

"My favorite trail used to be Willoughby," said Jessica. "But now it's often so crowded, and people just stop in the middle."

"Completely irritating!" agreed Griffin. "Gorgeous views, though."

"Yeah. Now I like Carriage Road to something, Dippers, maybe? And then you cut over so you come down right in front of the lodge to the lift, not that flat section at the bottom of the dippers."

"Yeah, I know what you mean., We did it a couple times last time we were up. It's fast and has a variety of narrow and wide."

"Uhhuh. And Carriage House sometimes gets pretty scraped off and icy, so it cuts down on the traffic."

"You just don't like crowds anywhere, do you?"

"Nope," laughed Jessica.

Thursday dawned with bright sun, blue skies, and a working furnace. It looked like a perfect day. Jessica made them bacon, while

Griffin made waffles. They packed water bottles, apples, cookies, and energy balls into their ski bags. They had talked about packing lunches, but it just wasn't as appetizing as wings at the bar when they wanted a break.

The first run they did was Willoughby. They weren't the first tracks on the mountain, but they were there within the first hour of it being open, so the corduroy from the groomers was still pretty fresh. Being near the end of the season, there was a lot of ice under the powder, but their sharp skis cut right over it. The next run they agreed to do East Bowl on the other side of the mountain. The trick with East Bowl was not to go too late in the day when the sun started to melt the snow and slow it down on the flat sections or you ended up trying to nordic ski in alpine skis - not handy. It did have some lovely jumps, and wound through the woods. It was another trail that didn't get a lot of traffic, not like Powder Horn or Deer Run. Next, they did Jessica's favorite, starting on Carriage House and ending right in front of the lodge.

"You ready for a break yet?" asked Griffin as they paused.

"I could take one, but I don't need it yet," answered Jessica.

"Good. Last one to the lift buys the first drink later!" called Griffin as he pushed off.

Jessica was just a hair's breadth behind him starting and hung right beside him on the swoop down to the lift. They agreed it was a tie as they waited for the chair to swing around and carry them back to the top of the mountain.

Turning to look behind them and the miles and miles of gorgeous view, Jessica asked, "Can we see the cabin from here?"

"Nah, I don't think so. Cause remember, we kinda wind up a hill and then set over it." He had turned to look, too. "See, it would be that road there from Rt 114, and we turn up there ish..." His voice trailed off as he tried to trace the route. "Yeah, no, you can't see it."

'That's too bad," said Jessica. "Look at all the gorgeous purples and blues though across the mountains right up to the deep blue sky with perfect, puffy white clouds."

"Perfect clouds in color and shape, but also 'cause there aren't hardly any."

"Right. It's like perfect weather. Cool enough to keep the snow in shape, but not so my face or fingers are cold."

"It's like the perfect ski day," agreed Griffin. "Tomorrow is supposed to be the same."

"Yeah?"

"Yeah."

Friday morning they both woke up a little stiff from skiing, but once they started moving around and took some Advil, they were both good to go and agreed to ski at least a half day.

They started with the same pattern of runs first with Willoughby and East Bowl early, but then they mixed in Bear Den, and the Shoot along with Powder Horn and some woods trails like Lew's Leap and Lee's Loop - though they kept messing up the names and ended up just calling them the First and Second trails.

By their midday break, they were both moving slowly and with tired backs. Neither of them had fallen at all except for catching edges on the woods trails and those weren't spectacular falls, more just heavy sit-downs.

They sat in the bar, with their boots unbuckled and hair messy.

Sipping her cider, Jessica said, "Y'know, I'll stay here as long as you want, either right here or on those couches by the fire, but I think I'm done for the day."

"Sore or tired?" asked Griffin.

"Yes," chuckled Jessica. "Both. I'm not hurting yet, but I'm going to be stiff tomorrow, I think."

"Uhhuh. I do know," grinned Griffin. "And you know, we're more likely to get hurt, like seriously hurt, if we push too far. We're not really in shape for this."

"No, we don't ski each weekend, or it would be different."

"No worries. We'll have lunch, hang out, and eventually meander back. We don't have a schedule. We can always ski more tomorrow or not."

"Yeah," Jessica chewed her lip as she thought. "I hate to waste the money of the full-day ticket for the rest of the day, but a broken leg would be a pain in the butt."

"No kidding," agreed Griffin. "We'll stay here tonight, and tomorrow we can ski again, or just hang out or head back. Now that the furnace is fixed, we don't have to stay longer. It's completely open."

"Yeah. I kinda like the idea of staying and just relaxing. You know if we go home, there will just be tasks that we decide to do."

"You're not wrong." Griffin thought about how Jessica was always working either meal prepping or writing or work-working. They both needed a break.

"We could always go to Littleton this evening for dinner. Or Newport or something. Maybe there's something playing at the movies."

"Yeah, look it up," agreed Jessica with a little yawn.

Griffin chuckled at her, "We could also go back and take a nap."

"We could do both," Jessica grinned.

"Sure."

After another drink with their orders of wings and a huge bowl of fries, Griffin and Jessica slowly packed up their stuff. Knees and lower backs agreed that it was time to be done for the week. "The good thing is that we don't have to take any of this ski stuff out of the car," said Jessica as they pulled into the cabin's driveway.

"You know," said Griffin, "that doesn't make me sad." They both laughed.

Inside, they slipped out of layers of sweatshirts, long johns, and extra socks. The Jessica lay on the living room rug to do some stretches and yoga poses.

Griffin couldn't help but watch and imagine her twisting around his body like that. "You're that sore?" he asked.

"Kinda. I can feel it tightening up. Especially my neck and shoulders."

"Here," Griffin said, "roll over on your belly. I'll rub your lower back. Then sit up and I'll do your shoulders."

"You don't have-"

"I know, shut up," Griffin cut off Jessica's arguments. "Besides," he added with a grin Jessica could feel in his voice, "you can rub me afterwards. I'm getting stiff too."

Jessica couldn't help but laugh, which Griffin noticed jiggled her butt in a rather appealing way. "Stop that, or I'll be too stiff to rub you."

Jessica continued to giggle, but soon changed to a deep moan as Griffin's hands melted away the stiffness from her lower back. Then he rubbed her thighs and butt, too.

"Sit up," Griffin said with a growl in his voice that melted Jessica to her core.

Jessica sat up, cross-legged, and Griffin began kneading her shoulders, easing the tension. She moaned again at the pleasure of it, melting under his hands.

"I love hearing you sound like that," Griffin whispered, his hot breath tickling her neck. "I would love it even more if you were moaning my name."

Then he began fluttering kisses along her neck. She tilted her head away, exposing more of her neck, and his hands moved lower and around her sides, cupping and gently massaging her breasts, too. He kissed her throat, and she tipped back her head to meet his lips. Her arms went up and held his head down as their lips parted and tongues danced.

Jessica gave a little nip to Griffin's lip and then said, "We should move upstairs."

"Why?" He mumbled back against her lips, "no one is here."

"No, but it's more comfortable."

"Hmm, true." He gave her another kiss and then pulled back. Standing, he reached a hand down to pull her up and then slipped his arms around her waist, pulling her against him, kissing her again.

"You are stiff," giggled Jessica. "I think I do need to rub you."

"Uhhmm, that sounds good," Griffin smiled, too. Then he pushed her towards the stairs. "You first, so I can watch that perfect ass ahead of me."

Chapter 21 - The week flew by

By Saturday afternoon, Jessica and Griffin decided to head back home so they could have a full day of rest before the new workweek. It also let them hang out for their weekly lunch with Mellie. She was a little jealous of their gorgeous skiing days, but not at all envious of waiting around for the furnace guys. They agreed to test Jessica the following weekend and help her prepare for her cooking competition. Mellie promised to bring random ingredients for Jessica to cook into three parts of a meal. Hopefully, it would be a good time for all.

Tuesday's morning work meeting brought some fun news. A client was so happy with the firm's work that they were all invited to attend a masquerade evening at the local "castle" just down the street from Jessica and Griffin's home. Apparently, Jessica wouldn't have to wait for summer to have a tour of the stunning building. The masquerade was a benefit for the children's wing of the local hospital, but their tickets would be purchased by the client - no strings attached.

"I've always wanted to go to a masquerade," said Jessica to one of the office girls. The entire floor was abuzz with the excitement even though it was a couple weeks away.

"What would you dress as?" asked Kara, her eyes wide with excitement.

"I don't know. There are so many themes we could go with," answered Jessica, equally excited. "I mean, the place looks like a castle, so we could easily dress like kings and queens with ornate crowns and masks. Or we could all go as something like...I don't know butterflies.'

"Ooh!" interrupted Kara, "If we all went as animals, that would be cool. Or an underwater theme and some people could be sharks or octopi and some could be mermaids."

"Sharks and mermaids," laughed Jessica. "Yes! I love it!"

"Just not during shark week," chuckled Lisa, another designer.

"Um, no. Let's keep it happy, not bloody," agreed Kara.

"You and Griffin could have matching masks and outfits."

"I am not twinning with him. That would look ridiculous."

"Ha! No, I meant you could follow the same theme," explained Kara, giggling.

Jessica laughed it off, but she thought the idea was cute. Actually, she liked the idea of their whole office following one general theme, like the underwater idea, but then couples could have something more tying them together.

"Ohhh, pirates would be fun!" exclaimed Kara.

"Hmm, that could be really fun. We could still have an entire sea/ocean theme. Mermaids, pirates, and octopi." The girls dissolved in giggles, but the thoughts were churning and soon there would be a plan. Jessica was sure of it.

Sure enough, a few minutes later, an email from Mike came through suggesting a shared theme for the office to attend the masquerade. He included a poll for favorite theme or subtheme ideas. Jessica filled in her opinions and then decided not to think about it anymore. Between work, her own stories, and this crazy cooking competition, she had more than enough to think about right now!

By Saturday, Jessica was a bag of nerves wondering what Mellie might bring for her secret cooking ingredient challenge. Griffin and she had been watching some episodes of *Chopped* during the week. Jessica realized that she really needed to kick up her seafood game, and so they had been experimenting some with that. Together they had made a shellfish pasta dish and a crab cake meal. Griffin remembered that she had made a seafood bisque before and told her she could always fall back on that. It was delicious. But now, they were actually a little sick of seafood.

Sunday chores were done, and Jessica couldn't focus. So she surprised Griffin by sitting down in front of the tv with a ball of yarn.

He blinked his eyes fast in confusion and scratched his chin. "Um, what?" He asked. "What are you doing? Knitting?"

Jessica chuckled. "Crocheting actually. I didn't have much yarn left, but I found this started cozy, so I thought it would be good to occupy me for a little."

Griffin couldn't quite adjust to this new hobby of Jessica's that he was discovering. "Cozy?" he asked.

"Yeah," Jessica chuckled again. "I've sold them online and at craft fairs. See, they're a cozy for pints of ice cream so you can eat it without your hands getting cold."

"No way!"

"Yes, way."

"I need one. I didn't know I needed one, but now I definitely need one." Griffin stood up. "In fact, I'll go buy us ice cream right now so we can use it."

"And in case my mystery dessert sucks."

"Well, that too." He grinned at her. "Kidding! You will not suck. But ice cream sounds really good right now, and Mellie won't be here for an hour or two. She's coming earlier than usual to give you time to cook, but I don't know exactly when."

"Yeah," Jessica smiled, "she just kinda shows up when she gets there."

"Uhhuh." Griffin was pulling on his boots. "What kind do you want?"

"Wait! You're actually getting ice cream?"

"Yeah."

"Umm," Jessica paused crocheting to look at him blankly. "I don't know. Something without nuts or, preferably, fruit either. Chocolate, coffee, and chocolate are always good."

"Ok, got it." Griffin popped out the door and the house was suddenly too quiet.

Jessica grabbed her phone to put on an audio book, but scrolling through her library, none of them sounded good, or they were way too long to start for just a half hour listening session. She flipped on the tv instead. "Sure, let's do more *Chopped* research." Jessica grimaced and yet was a little excited, too. She probably had enough yarn to finish this ice cream cozy and another one. It wasn't her intent to make them matching ice cream cozies, but apparently she was now. She would need more yarn to make one for Mellie, too, but there wasn't enough time this weekend, anyway.

Chapter 22 - Open the bag, please.

It was almost like *Chopped*. Mellie had brought three bags of ingredients and handed the first one to Jessica. "First up is an appetizer. Take a look at today's mystery ingredients!"

Jessica laughed nervously. "Ok, here's the deal. I'm going to do this stupid game with your stupid ingredients that I bet are going to be impossible. But we're not doing a countdown timer. Just time me to see how long I take and I'll try to be as fast as possible."

"You sure?" asked Griffin.

"That's not how it works," added Mellie.

"Yeah, I can only handle so much stress at a time. If I let you do this to me again, we can set a real timer." Jessica was already sweating.

"Fair enough," agreed Griffin.

"Good. Look in the bag then for your ingredients." Mellie was no longer in the best friend role, but instead in the competition judge role. "Remember, you must use them all."

Jessica peeked into the bag and then pulled out the secret ingredients. She pulled out taco shells, cream cheese, jalapenos, and cherries.

"What the hell, Mellie?" Jessica looked over at her in consternation.

"What can I say? I tried to be random in a 'maybe it can go together' way." Mellie shrugged and grinned.

"Ugh." Jessica bit her lip and thought. She could do a stuffed jalapeno with everything except the cherries. What was she gonna do with those? She decided to start halving the jalapenos and removing the seeds while she thought. She also threw the shells under the broiler to crisp them up.

"I have no idea what you're gonna do with this," chuckled Griffin.

"A mess, probably," answered Jessica with a depreciating chuckle. Then she melted a little bit of butter in a pan. The idea of a dipping sauce came to mind for the cherries, so she began chopping them up finely.

"Don't forget the shells," offered Mellie.

"Yup." Jessica bit her lip as she finished chopping the last cherries. She dumped the pits into the trash and then grabbed the shells out of the oven. She dropped the shells onto a plate and dropped the hot baking sheet into the sink. Checking the butter to be sure it wasn't burning, she took another plate and crushed the shells between the two plates until they were just small crumbs. She dumped those into the butter, added salt, and a spicy maple seasoning. She quickly browned the crumbs as she simmered the cherries in a little of orange juice and a lot of sugar. She added a splash of apple vinegar and some more of that spicy maple seasoning. She dumped the crumbs onto the plate from earlier and then chopped up some cooked leftover bacon and cilantro that they had in the fridge. She whipped together the cream cheese, bacon, and cilantro in a small bowl. Jessica took a small spoon and stuffed each jalapeno with the cream cheese mixture. Then she topped it with the golden crumbs and popped them back into the oven.

"I think I timed that wrong. I maybe should have microwaved the peppers a little, or pre-baked them. They won't cook through in time." Jessica said that as she checked her sauce. It was a little sweet and a little spicy - perfect.

"Learning time, that's what this practice session is for. You'll know that next time." Griffin smiled. "I'm amazed how quickly you did all of this."

"She always has been organized. You should have seen her multitask in a science lab. Her notes were always the best, too." Mellie laughed and stuck out her tongue at Jessica.

"Stop!" laughed Jessica, relaxing. "You're making me sound like a wicked nerd."

"Aren't you?"

"Maybe."

Jessica pulled out the peppers and plated them. Then she dribbled just a few drops of the sauce on each popper and set the rest in a little bowl for dipping.

"Oh. My. God." said Griffin a moment later through a mouthful of popper. "This is soooo good."

"This is fucking amazing, Jessica," added Mellie.

"But it wouldn't matter because I wouldn't have gotten it on the plate," argued Jessica.

"Gee, you weren't perfect the first time?" ribbed Mellie. "Ok, so seriously, you would have served them like this. Just the peppers wouldn't have been quite soft enough. The flavors would have been all there, so maybe you would have lost a point or two for not being cooked completely, but you still would have rocked it."

"Yup!" agreed Griffin. "This is amazing, and I want more."

"They are pretty good," admitted Jessica, wiping a drip of the sauce from the corner of her mouth.

"Ok, clean up, then the next round," said Mellie. "You get out for a minute and refocus." She kicked Jessica out of the kitchen.

"Time on the clock, let's start," said Griffin a few minutes later, in his best tv announcer voice.

In the next bag were pork chops on the bone, tiny purple potatoes, parsnips, and large mushrooms. Jessica blew a strand of hair out of her face and turned to the fridge. She pulled out cream, butter, and a hard cider. "Open that," she said to Griffin, sliding it across the counter to him. Then she turned to the cabinet and pulled out several spices, and salt and pepper, of course.

Jessica took a gulp of the cider.

"I don't think you can drink during the competition, hun," said Mellie.

"Nope, probably not. But I'm still home right now," laughed Jessica, blowing that strand of hair out of her eyes again.

Jessica began by patting dry the pork chops. Then she mixed the spices together and liberally coated both sides of each chop. She set a pan on the stove and added a pat of butter to it, but didn't turn it on quite yet. Then she set a pot of water on and turned it to boil. She moved to peeling and roughly chopping the parsnips and purple potatoes, which she added to the water as it began to simmer. She sliced the mushrooms in large pieces and pulled another frying pan out. Another slab of butter went into that pan as she finely sliced some onion. "Y'all are doing the dishes, right?" Jessica looked up with a grin. She stepped back for a moment and reset her ponytail and then washed her hands again.

Jessica tossed the onion and mushroom into the pan and let them caramelize. At the same time, she turned the first pan of butter on. She stirred the potatoes and parsnips. Then she pulled salad greens, a carrot, and a tomato out of the fridge. She deftly made a quick salad, removed the onion and mushrooms to a bowl, and then set the pork chops into the hot butter to sear them. Flipping the chops to sear the other sides, she set about making a gravy in the onion/mushroom pan. She poured in a little chicken stock, because that was what she had. "Think their kitchen will be better stocked?" Jessica asked.

"Probably," Griffin said, handing her a second cider.

"Thanks." Jessica blew a huff of air up her face and gulped some more cider. She turned down the chop's heat and covered them. Then she drained the potatoes and parsnips. She added them back to the pot, added cream, butter, salt, and pepper, and used the hand blender to mash them. She soon had a gorgeous purple mash. It wasn't thin like a puree, but the texture of normal mashed potatoes, but they were a pretty purple. She checked the flavor, since parsnips were not her norm.

The pork chops were the big question then. She needed them cooked through, but didn't want them dry. She flipped them again, to recrust the top that had collected moisture from the lid. Then she pulled it off the heat and onto a cutting board to rest.

She plated with a flare of purple potato mash, a side salad, and a chop with the mushrooms and onions on top with a side of gravy..

"Ok, I guess. I'm not sure if the pork is actually cooked all the way, but I don't want to overcook them," said Jessica as she laid plates in front of Mellie and Griffin. She moved dirty dishes to the sink, soaking the empty pans before she stood to have her own. "You're not seriously taking a picture of it?"

"Of course I am!" argued Mellie. "This looks gorgeous!"

"Actually, send us each a copy, too. We might use it for graphics sometime," said Griffin as he cut a piece of the pork chop. It appeared perfectly cooked, white through the center, but still juicy. He dipped it into the purple mash and popped it into his mouth. "Oh dayum!"

"It's ok?" asked Jessica nervously.

"Oh, it's more than ok. Mellie put away your phone and eat. Try this, Jessica."

It was really good. And they cleared the plates once Jessica grabbed some dressing from the fridge. "I didn't time it right to make a dressing."

"No, but this is stupendously good, and you finished at 39 minutes. So you should be ok on time if it's 40 and if it's 45, you would have had time for an oil dressing."

"True."

Chapter 23 - Dessert

"Whew! I don't know if I have it in me to do dessert," said Jessica. "This is hard."

"Yeah it is," agreed Mellie. "This is amazing. I can't believe you signed up for this."

"Yeah, about that-" started Griffin.

"Ha!" laughed Jessica. "Me too."

"Huh?" Mellie looked between them, confused.

"Yeah, so Jessica didn't sign up for it," said Griffin.

"What do you mean? You're not doing it?"

"Oh no, she is," clarified Griffin, "but she didn't sign up. I did."

"You can't cook!" laughed Mellie.

"No, I mean," said Griffin, "I signed her up. She didn't volunteer for this."

"Ohhh," Mellie leaned back, grinning. "Yeah, that makes more sense."

"Yeah," was all that Jessica said while shooting a glare at Griffin.

"Hmm," said Mellie, "You don't have to do it just 'cause he signed you up for it, but I bet you'll kick butt."

"Definitely!" agreed Griffin.

"Maybe." Jessica took a deep breath. "Ok, let's see what hellacious items you brought for dessert."

Jessica opened the last bag and set the mystery ingredients onto the counter. There were chocolate mint candies, peaches, maple syrup - the real stuff, and day old, plain donuts.

Griffin just started to laugh.

"What the hell, Mellie?" asked Jessica, perplexed.

"Day old donuts," chortled Griffin.

"I wonder if I can slice them?" muttered Jessica as she pulled out a cutting board and paring knife.

"What?" asked Mellie.

"We'll see," said Jessica. "But I transformed your stupid taco shells by making them crumbs, so I feel like I should try something else right now. We'll see if we can slice the donuts, but if not, maybe I can turn it into some sort of flour and sugar batter...I don't know."

"I never would have thought of that," said Mellie.

"Yeah, there's a reason for that. No one cooks with old donuts."

Jessica carefully sliced the donuts into little rounds. "Ok, I'm not sure whether I'm baking them or frying them, but ok."

She was thinking about the chocolate mints while she sliced. That was the tricky part. The maple syrup and peaches could work in lots of ways.

"Oh!"

"You have an idea?" asked Griffin.

"Yeah," grinned Jessica. "This could be cool."

She dumped the candies and some butter on a low heat to melt. Then she tossed the donut rounds onto a baking sheet and tossed them under the broiler. "Don't let me forget those."

She placed the cream in the freezer, then began chopping up the peaches.

Griffin sat back in awe as he watched Jessica create pudding from scratch with the maple syrup and peaches for flavor. As that set, she dipped the now cooled donut circles into the melted chocolate mint candies. She dipped them so they were half covered and half bare.

"Oh! Brilliant!" Griffin was blown away by the creativity.

"Yeah, well," replied Jessica, "we'll see how it tastes."

Jessica served them each a bowl of warm pudding with a peach slice on top and chocolate-covered donut circles arranged at the side. "If I had either fresh mint or fresh raspberries, I think they would be a nice garnish, too."

"Hmmm, that would be pretty," agreed Mellie.

"So, I've never made pudding from scratch before. The idea I had was ice cream-"

"Oh, that would have been perfect!"

"Right, so pudding is kinda close, but the donut things would be better with ice cream, I think."

"Eh, I think it will be good, no matter what."

Jessica handed them each a spoon, and they dug in."

"Oh. These are the best day old donuts ever," said Mellie. "Maybe we should do this on the regular. Bake them and add a coating."

"Right?" agreed Griffin, "and this pudding is really good."

"I wonder if it would have been better cold instead of served warm."

"I dunno."

Jessica began giggling then.

"What?" asked Griffin.

"I hate peach yogurt and then I made peach pudding."

"Yeah, but it works."

Jessica looked around the kitchen. Even with Mellie and Griffin washing dishes between each round, it was a mess. Her shoulders slumped looking at it.

Mellie caught the look. "Hey girl, you're not cleaning up. We are. Go sit."

"Are you sure?" asked Jessica, feeling a little guilty.

"Yeah, go sit. Take some of these yummy chocolate mint donut things to munch on."

"Curl up with a book or your crocheting," added Griffin,

"You still crochet?" asked Mellie with a huge smile. "I almost asked you to make me something."

"Oh, yeah?" asked Jessica in a tired voice.

"Uhhuh. But not today. It's just a fun thing, so I'll ask you later. Rest now, you earned that. You did good!"

Chapter 24 - Masquerade

Jessica and Griffin often walked their neighborhood or walked along the beach. Either way, they usually walked past the grand house down at the end of the block. It really did look like a castle. It had granite stonework behind a wrought-iron fence. The house was just off a private beach, and because of this, the salt air had caused a rusty patina on the wrought iron fences and gates, making them look like dark walnut from a distance. But it was the two towers on the corners of the house that really gave it personality. There was a long balcony stretching between the towers and the house behind them. It was a gorgeous house/mansion and perfect for a masquerade party fundraiser.

Jessica wasn't much of a shopper. She shopped primarily for comfort and practicality. Which meant she did not have a ball gown handy or any sort of costume for a masquerade. She wasn't sure if it was better or worse when they were given the theme from the office. As an entire group, they would go with a fairy tale characters. That left it really wide open. Kara was going as either Little Bo Peep or Alice in Wonderland - neither was exactly a fairytale, but close enough. Mellie thought that Jessica and Griffin should go as Little Red Riding Hood and the Wolf, but Griffin said he would only consider it if he was the woodsman. Jessica wanted something more in a fantasy line like elves, but wanted to stay far away from princesses. Shopping was tough.

Jessica had spent the week scrolling through online stores looking for a costume, or pieces to create a costume, and Pinterest for inspiration. On Friday night, Jessica and Mellie left work early to hit some actual stores. Finally, Jessica had outfits for herself and Griffin.

Sitting at a greasy burger place, Jessica was relieved to be done shopping. She sipped her coffee, trying to regain her sanity.

Jessica had settled on a version of Little Red Riding Hood that she was writing. It wasn't a published story yet, but a retelling of a famous story. So it met the requirements of a familiar fairy tale and Jessica's desire for elfish magic. Griffin thought it was a cool twist.

Jessica had a gorgeous dress of blues and greens with a hint of shimmer and the idea of leaves embroidered in. Little seed pearls and embroidery added flowers along the bottom, the sleeves, and an accent like a belt. Tiny, tiny bells were sewn into the dress, leaving a trail of soft musical notes as Jessica moved. Her mask covered one cheek, over her eyes, and up over her forehead. It was dark green leaves with dainty pink flowers. It circled around her head, giving the impression of a flower crown and had tiny vines that hung down the back with her long brown hair.

Griffin was able to wear dress clothes he already had, along with a brown leather vest. Jessica suggested he should go shirtless and just wear the vest. Unfortunately, it wasn't a summer party, so it seemed unlikely. The leather vest had an embossing of leaves and vines and had a subtle elegance matching Jessica's dress. His mask was mostly golden, in a masculine type of lacework on brown leather. It sounded heavy when Jessica described it over the phone, but Griffin was happy to feel how lightweight it actually was. At a craft store they found some leaves and little vine to add onto the edges of it to tie it into the theme better.

They found a piece of costume jewelry of a giant ruby choker and matching bracelet and earrings for Jessica. They eventually ordered a faux wood cutting ax for Griffin. They added a belt he could hang the plastic ax off of so he wouldn't have to hold it except for photos. He looked like a rugged woodsman and Jessica's stomach had butterflies as she looked at them together, reflected in the dark window as they were dressed for the night. Later, those butterflies returned when she looked at pictures from the night.

"Ready m'lady?" Griffin gave an outlandish bow as he asked Jessica if she was ready to leave.

She laughed so hard she could hardly answer. "For sure, my rugged outdoorsman. But I need you to protect me from all the terrible monsters tonight."

"Of course, m'lady. I have my trusty wood ax here and these brawny muscles." Griffin broke down in laughter then, unable to keep up the act. "Seriously though. Would you like to walk because it isn't far, or ride over because these shoes aren't really winter walking shoes?"

"It seems silly to drive such a short distance, but I'm not sure we want to wear boots and change."

"No. We'll drive."

Jessica grabbed a red shawl. It was as close to a red hooded robe as she could find that wasn't totally cheesy. "I'm not going to bring a coat though. We're so close."

"Right." Griffin appraised her outfit and loved it. He could imagine a version of this in lingerie, and it made him want to skip the masquerade altogether.

Moments later, they pulled into line for the mansion. A valet took their keys, and they joined the quickly moving crowd climbing the front steps. A coat check was just inside the doors, and then several servers with flutes of champagne and sweet wines. Griffin took two flutes and handed one to Jessica. "May our evening be magical," he toasted.

"I'm sure it will," replied Jessica.

The grand ballroom of the historic mansion glowed with a soft, sparkling light from chandeliers adorned with crystal teardrops. The room was gorgeous, draped in rich, burgundy velvet curtains and golden embellishments. The comfortable furniture around the edges of the room were deep brown leather or soft red velvet as well. The guests, in a stunning array of elaborate costumes, swirled across the floor to the strains of a classical orchestra, their laughter mingling with music.

Small, tall tables were scattered about with appetizers, and servers wove through the crowd offering drinks, taking empty glasses, and offering more bite sized nibbles.

In the midst of this spectacle, Jessica and Griffin made their entrance, immediately drawing the eye of everyone present. Jessica had embraced the role of Red Riding Hood with enchanting grace. The silver on her ears hinted at the elfin twist she was using, but it wasn't overt. Her dress fit her perfectly, and the mask teased her beautiful face. Griffin, equally captivating, stood as the embodiment of the Woodsman. His attire was a masterful blend of rugged and refined. His mask showed off his piercing eyes, which hardly moved off from Jessica as she was looking around breathlessly. She loved this scene.

As they moved through the crowd, Jessica and Griffin were the epitome of a storybook romance. They danced gracefully, their movements synchronized as though they were characters in a well-rehearsed ballet. Jessica's laughter was like the chime of delicate bells, while Griffin's deep voice rumbled like a majestic waterfall, each complementing the other in perfect harmony. The pair drew admiring glances and whispered conversations. Their costumes stood out amidst the myriad of fantasy characters that filled the room. They quickly found the rest of the office staff and, after the first two songs, they danced their way over to the group.

"You two look like a marvelous version of a common fairy tale," said Mike, looking them over. "You should have had me dress like the Big Bad Wolf and we could have been a thruple."

A blond woman next to him lightly punched him in the arm. "And what about me?" she laughed. "Well, I didn't think you wanted to be a grandmother, so I was going to let you continue being the princess."

"Maybe you should be a wolf and not a frog," laughed the blond, obviously amused. "Then I could lock you in the doghouse. No kisses needed."

"Oh hey, now!" Mike didn't have an immediate comeback, and the entire group laughed.

The atmosphere was electric, charged with the enchantment of the masquerade and the palpable chemistry between Jessica and Griffin. As they twirled beneath the sparkling chandeliers, it was as if they had stepped out of a fairy tale and into the heart of a dream, their costumes bringing to life the magic of their roles.

"I'm exhausted and completely peopled out, but I don't want the evening to end," sighed Jessica after a couple of hours.

"I know what you mean," agreed Griffin. "If only we could bring this feeling back with us, but just sit down and chill for a while."

"Exactly."

"Why don't we take a peek up in the tower? I overheard someone say it's open. I think we can look out over the town and the ocean. I bet the view is nice."

"Oh!" Jessica had forgotten about the towers. "That sounds amazing. Let's do it."

It took only a moment to climb the curved stairs, and suddenly they were alone in the quiet. Through the high, arched window, the late winter night stretched out in a gorgeous, panoramic view. The town below was cloaked in a soft, deep darkness, punctuated by the soft, golden glow from windows and highlighted by the blueish shine from streetlights. A breeze snuck in through a window cracked open. The air outside was crisp and still, carrying with it the faint scent of ocean salt and the sharp, clean tang of winter.

Beyond the town, the ocean stretched out in a vast, shadowy expanse. Its surface was a dark, inky indigo, broken only by the occasional glint of moonlight that dancing upon the slowly moving waves. It gave a general appearance that the tide was moving out, but Jessica got a little dizzy staring at it, trying to decide which way the tide was moving.

"Careful now." Griffin's hand was warm against her back and steadied her. "I do the same thing sometimes," he said, staring out at the water. "I think it's going out. What about you?"

"I think so too. That's how it feels," Jessica replied, steadier now.

The moon, a silvery crescent, hung low in the sky, casting a ghostlike luminance over the scene. The sky itself was a deep blue, almost black, studded with distant, sparkling stars that seem to pinpoint with a quiet, tiny brilliance. Just a little frost etched around the edges of the window, framing this beautiful view.

The peacefulness of the scene invited a sense of reflection and calm, as the quiet of the night and the gentle sounds of the ocean wove together into a tapestry of serene winter nightfall. "This is amazing," Jessica said.

"Uhhmmm," agreed Griffin.

"I wish we could come here all the time."

"Imagine what it would be like during a storm?"

"Oh, the waves crashing as the wind whips the water and thunder crashing all around?"

"Uhhuh," Griffin grinned. "It would be amazing!"

"Yeah, it would."

Chapter 25 - The Competition

Saturday morning was typically a day that Jessica would stay in bed until 8-9 or get up and have breakfast and then lounge around for a few hours. But this weekend, she woke up at 4:30 and couldn't shut off her brain. Finally, around 6 she gave up. She left a note on the counter and then slipped out to go to the gym. She was full of nervous energy and decided to channel it.

Griffin texted her around 7:30: Nervous?

Jessica: Yup.

Jessica: Just finishing up. I'll be home to shower and dress, then we need to leave before too long.

Griffin: Nah, we don't need to leave until about 9, but you need to eat, too.

Jessica: I don't think I can.

Griffin: :) we'll have you eat something light.

Jessica: B there shortly

Griffin was in the living room when Jessica came in. "Take your shower," he said. "I'll make coffee when I hear the water shut off."

"You're awesome." Jessica grinned at him. Excluding the fact that he had signed her up for this stupid competition in the first place, he was a sweet guy.

The shower soothed Jessica, just as using the equipment at the gym had, but the nervous energy was back as she got dressed. She chose clothes that were lightweight and easily moveable, so she wouldn't be hampered as she cooked. She also purposely chose short sleeves. Then she pulled her hair back in a high ponytail to keep her neck cool. She braided it, so she wouldn't have to worry about stray hairs falling into the food. She had a bandana that she carried down with her phone. She might want it later in the kitchens, she hadn't decided.

Griffin slid a mug of coffee over the counter to her. He had chopped up some fruit and cooked bacon. "Toast?" he asked. Griffin wanted her to eat so she had energy, but was keeping it light and food she could eat with her fingers.

"Umm, sure." Jessica crunched on a piece of bacon. "Thank you."

"Of course." Griffin paused for a moment, then asked, "Wanna talk or wanna sit quietly? I don't know how to help you. I've never seen you stressed before."

Jessica laughed softly. "Yeah, I don't know." She stretched her neck from side to side. "I mean, I wish I could just get started, y'know. This waiting is the hardest part."

"Yeah." Griffin understood. He hated hurrying up and waiting for anything. Even waiting for the furnace repair guys had kinda sucked because he didn't know a timeframe and couldn't make plans, even though there was no rush for anything there. "Ok, so let's eat and then we can head over. You can scope out your competitors while you wait and maybe see what the kitchens are like. That'll help, right? A few less unknowns."

Jessica flashed him a huge smile. "For sure!" She held her coffee with intention and smelled it, letting the comforting vapors soothe her. Then she popped some melon into her mouth. "I mean, the worst-case scenario is that I'm the first one eliminated, and since I didn't even sign up for this, it doesn't really mean anything. Right?"

"Sure, that sounds reasonable." Griffin was sure she wouldn't be the first out. He was confident she would make at least the middle eliminations, but it really depended on the other chefs and what was in the baskets.

Griffin drove to the hotel conference center where the competition was being held. It was a good thing, because Jessica was so deep in thinking about recipes, she probably would have missed the exit and the next turn. The next hour was a whirlwind of being directed where to go, being assigned an apron and a cooking station. She got to choose a bandana color, one of four. Apparently, her thought to bring one made sense, but now she had a snazzy new one with the competition logo. She didn't know if the colors were important, but she went with the pastel blue because blue was her favorite color.

And then it started.

Honestly, Jessica couldn't even remember the first two rounds at all. Every station and contestant was buzzing with energy and the scent of stress was almost more powerful than the aromas of foods cooking. The ridiculously bright lights reflected off the sleek countertops, and the clatter of pots and pans filled the air, punctuated by sizzling oils and blenders grinding. There was a crash as someone dropped a dish and then a call for a medic for a cut. Jessica hardly glanced up. She had done alright in the first two rounds, the appetizers. She was not, in fact, any of the first four eliminated, but now there were only two chefs with the pale blue bandanas. They both wore them rolled and wrapped around their forehead to capture the sweat before it rolled into their eyes.

Jessica rubbed her face on the inside of her elbow, unsatisfactory, but better than nothing while keeping her hands clean.

One judge called out, "Alright, chefs! We're down to the wire. You've got just five minutes left to put the finishing touches on your dishes."

Jessica's hands were a blur as she carefully plated a delicate arrangement of seared scallops, a vibrant saffron risotto, and a bright spinach citrus salad. The dish was an ambitious fusion of Italian and Mediterranean flavors, reflecting her passion for bold and fresh ingredients. She had practiced with scallops and loved risotto, so she thought it would be good. The spinach salad infused with citrus wedges and citrus vinaigrette would offer the perfect counterpart to the fish and seafood, she hoped.

One of the female judges, Jessica had quickly forgotten her name, stood close. "Jessica, can you tell us about the inspiration behind your dish?"

Jessica gulped air and wiped her face against her forearm again. "Of course! I've always loved the combination of citrus and seafood, so I wanted to highlight that in a refined way. The scallops are seared, and the saffron risotto adds a creamy depth. The spinach citrus salad is meant to bring a fresh, bright contrast."

Another judge had listened too. "Sounds wonderful. How do you feel about the balance of flavors?"

Jessica paused anxiously, then she said, "I think it's coming together. I'm a little worried that the risotto might not be as creamy as I'd like it to be. But I've been tasting and adjusting as I go, so I hope it's okay."

The woman spoke again. "Well, you've certainly got a lot of elements on the plate. Let's see if you can pull it all together."

Jessica gave a determined nod and took a deep breath. She carefully finished plating her dish, garnishing it with a sprinkle of micro greens and a drizzle of citrus vinaigrette. She placed one raspberry on a spinach leaf on the edge of the salad. It gave a pop of color and melded well with the salad flavors.

The timer buzzed loudly. Jessica stepped back and surveyed her creation with a mix of pride and apprehension. The judges approached her station, and the atmosphere grew tense.

"Let's see what you've got," said the friendlier male judge.

The woman, who had seemed so judgemental, took the first bite, her expression thoughtful. The friendlier judge followed suit, nodding appreciatively as he tasted the dish. The third judge took his turn, his face inscrutable as he savored the flavors.

The friendlier judge finally spoke, "Jessica, your scallops are beautifully seared, and the risotto has a lovely flavor. The citrus salad adds a nice brightness. But... the risotto could use a touch more creaminess to balance out the texture."

The woman smiled warmly and said, "I agree. The concept is fantastic, and you've executed it with great finesse. It's a delightful dish with just a few tweaks needed."

The third judge added, "You've done a commendable job. Your attention to detail is evident and the flavors are well thought out."

Jessica's knees nearly gave out as she heard the feedback. She beamed with relief and gratitude. "Thank you so much. I'll definitely take the feedback to heart."

The judges moved on to the next station, and Jessica let out a deep breath, her shoulders relaxing. She watched as the judges spoke with the other contestants, feeling a mixture of pride and nervous anticipation as the competition heated up.

The contestants were again sent out of the room as their stations were cleared and cleaned. Jessica guzzled water and jiggled her leg nervously until they were called back in. She thought she had done well, but everyone she could see had had beautiful dishes.

The host took his time, building the anticipation, but finally Jessica was relieved not to hear her name called. She had made it through another round.

Finally, Jessica made it to the sixth and final round, the dessert of her choice. They were down to the final four contestants. She couldn't believe that she would make it this far. She didn't know it, but Griffin had sent out a message to several of their friends, so a group from work, Mellie, and someone from the gym had joined him to watch the last couple of rounds.

Jessica was exhausted, both mentally and physically. She decided it was likely that one of the other contestants would do something super fancy or technical and pull it off. She figured that someone else would also go for broke, but not quite pull it off. She wasn't going to risk it. Jessica decided to go for something familiar and fairly easy, but satisfyingly good. She had been using the same chocolate chip cookie recipe for years and could do it without even measuring. She started that as she decided whether to do warm pudding or try ice cream to go with it.

Suddenly, she got the idea to create cookie bowls and the regular cookies. Trying that new thing convinced her to do pudding versus ice cream. So she started heating the milk in the stove and then began whisking together the sugar, cornstarch, and salt together in a small bowl while mixing the flour, sugars, salt, etc in the mixing bowl that she had beaten the butter, vanilla, and eggs in. Once the cookie dough batter was mixed, she tossed it in the freezer and then greased the outside of a jumbo muffin tin. By then she could slowly add the pudding ingredients into the warm milk, as her oven preheated. The comforting smells soothed her. Familiar had been the right choice.

Pulling out the cookie dough, she deftly spooned 12 balls of it onto parchment paper and slid it into the oven. After stirring the pudding resting on warm, she molded cookie dough around the outside of the muffin cups, careful to try to keep the mixture at an even thickness. Then she slid it into the oven beside the other pan.

Stirring the pudding again, Jessica then hurried over to the pantry area to find the perfect plates to show off her dessert. She grabbed a small bunch of violets, too.

Jessica pulled the cookies out of the oven and popped the muffin tin into the cooler to hasten the cooling process.

"Five minutes," boomed a judge's voice. Jessica hoped that they wouldn't come over again asking questions. They didn't every round, just sometimes, and her nerves were ragged now.

She began breaking the blossoms off the violets so she could set a blossom on top of each bowl of vanilla pudding and tuck one beside the bowl on the white, oval plate.

With only two minutes to spare, Jessica quickly and very delicately slid the cookie cups off the muffin tin. Then she filled each cookie cup two-thirds full with the vanilla pudding. She placed two chocolate chip cookies beside the bowl and tucked the flower under them to just barely peek out. A violet blossom was set in the center of each cup of pudding.

Jessica hesitated. She had enough cookies to tuck one into the pudding, but was that too much, or an appropriate add on? She bit her lip and wiped her face against the inside of her elbow.

"Twenty seconds."

Simple was better, Jessica decided, and she double checked that each plate was spotless and bereft of fingerprints.

The countdown timer buzzed, and relief coursed through Jessica. There was nothing else she needed to do except listen as the judges tasted. It was at that moment that she became aware of a large group in the crowd that seemed focused on her. Jessica flushed bright red as she realized all the people who had come to watch her. With a crooked smile she mouthed "I hate you," at Griffin.

He laughed and gave her a cheesy smile and thumbs up. Mellie laughed at them both.

Jessica had been right, one contestant had gone all out with truffles and pulled sugar, and Jessica had no idea how it all had been accomplished in thirty minutes. Another contestant had tried to make mini cheesecakes, berry glaze, and something else. It was good, but there were technical errors. The other two of them had gone for comfort desserts. The third contestant had made mini apple tarts, a berry glaze, and whipped cream.

Apparently, the judges preferred well made comfort desserts over almost perfect fancy food. The above-the-top chef took first place, and the apple tarts took third. Jessica was blown away when she and the fourth contestant both stepped forward for final judgment and she wasn't the one sent home! The applause for the winners was thunderous and Jessica was half convinced she misunderstood.

Until Griffin was at her side and wrapping her in a bear hug. "I knew you would kick butt!" he said.

Jessica met Mellie's eyes and whispered, "What the frick? What just happened?"

"What happened?" repeated Mellie. "What happened is that you proved what we have been saying. You're an awesome cook!"

Then her coworkers and friends crowded around and congratulated Jessica. Her hand tingled after an especially exuberant high five from Mike, who had gotten there just before the final judgements.

"Nice!" said Griffin, looking at the medal Jessica was awarded. Think you can get us free drinks at a bar?"

"Yeah no," laughed Jessica. "I'm exhausted. I'm going home to sit down and get off my feet. You can take it to a bar, though."

They all laughed, and most of them wished her more congratulations, well wishes, and that they would see her on Monday. Finally, it was just the three of them left. Mellie and Griffin helped Jessica carry her prizes out, which included a new set of pots and pans as well as an espresso maker. "Careful when you carry this in the house," said Mellie. "It looks like this might be a gift card in this top pot."

"Ok," said Jessica in a tired voice. She was a weird mix of amped energy and utter exhaustion.

"I think when we get home," said Griffin, "that our second-place winner here is going to take a nap and then we'll do pizza and ice cream for dinner."

"Yup, that sounds perfect," agreed Jessica. "Wanna join us, Mel?"

"Hmm, maybe. I'm already here. We could do that today and skip our weekly, tomorrow. I do gotta do laundry and stuff."

"Perfect."

Chapter 26 - A Few Months Later

"**I** can't believe your sister is getting married," said Jessica.

"I know," Griffin grinned back. "I feel like they've been together for ages, but I just didn't see her as the marrying kind."

"Nope. I thought she would always keep an escape route or the flexibility to just up and move chasing a new career dream or whatever."

"Or just up and move to new scenery. That sounds like her, too."

Griffin and Jessica were sitting back at the table after dinner and dishes. Mellie's fancy gold-leafed wedding invitation was peeking out of the faintly rose-colored envelope.

Griffin finished his beer and asked, "She's not pregnant, is she?"

"Not as far as I know." Jessica blinked, as the idea hadn't occurred to her. Would that be a reason for her bestie to get married?

"Well, you would be the first to know." Griffin shrugged and added, "You would probably even know before the dad to be."

Jessica laughed, "Yeah, probably. No, she hasn't mentioned being pregnant and last I knew, she wanted to wait a while."

Griffin paused a half moment before standing up to recycle his bottle. "Yeah, have you two talked about kids much?"

"Oh, heck no." Jessica laughed, "It came up while I was switching jobs, and how it's easier to make big changes when it's just yourself, not a whole family."

Griffin nodded, then realized that Jessica wasn't looking at him and said. "Got it. That's true." Then he added, "I always mean to travel more. I mean, now is the easiest time to do it, young and carefree. Plus, the job makes it easy. I can do a lot of it from anywhere, and yet I don't."

"Don't what?" Jessica had been distracted by messaging Mellie: *You're not pregnant, are you?*

"Oh, traveling." Jessica caught back up in the present conversation. "Yeah, I always want to travel and then never set it up. And you're right, we can work from anywhere with at least some internet. Let's go somewhere!"

"Ok!" Griffin was energized by the idea and took two more bottles out of the fridge. "We talked about Ireland, Australia, Mesoamerican ruins. Where else?"

"Hmm," Jessica bit her lip in thought. Her phone dinged, and she looked down. A series of laughing emojis and then *Hell no!*

Jessica: *I didn't think so. But Griffin asked, and I thought there was a slim possibility...*

Mellie: *hit him in the shoulder for me. Tell him not yet, but I expect him to be the godfather someday.*

"Not pregnant," Jessica said out loud. "And I'm supposed to slug you in the shoulder for suggesting it. Then tell you that you're going to be the godfather someday."

"Right," Griffin chuckled. That sounded just like his sister.

"So, let's pick a big trip to save for and something smaller right off," Jessica tried to be practical. "Oh!"

"Oh? Oh what?" asked Griffin.

"I always wanted to go on a cruise." She grinned. "I wonder if there are any sales soon?"

"A cruise could be fun. Especially a warm one."

"Uhhuh." She furrowed her brow. "But didn't you say you wanted to go to Norway, too? I think there are cruises that go there. We could tour, hit other places in Europe and be back."

"Let's do both."

Jessica blinked at him in confusion and opened the fresh bottle of cider he had grabbed her, sliding her empty one across the table to him. He obligingly recycled it and came back to sit down again. "Let's do a warm cruise and a cruise trip to Norway or along the European rivers - I swear I've seen that advertised. We can hit Ireland on the way home."

"Oh, that could be cool." Jessica pulled open a tab on her phone. Cruises leave all the time from Boston and New York, right? Those are easy to get to."

"Yeah, I think," replied Griffin.

The rest of the evening was spent looking up cruise packages and daydreaming. They did find a fun 10 day cruise that was a roundtrip from New York and went to the Caribbean. They made sure that there was internet so they could work also, and they wouldn't even need to take vacation time, saving that instead for a big trip to Europe in August or September.

Soon enough, they were pulling into the parking just off the docks. They had found a package deal for secure parking for just $10 a day. $100 for parking right by the ship and their car would be in a gated and guarded lot? Unheard of! Plus, both Jessica and Griffin were practical packers, so they each carried their work stuff in a backpack, had a small suitcase with clothes, and another small carryon with a few more outfits and daily necessities. Griffin laughed at Jessica for bringing a half dozen books, too.

"I don't want to be reading on my phone by the pool. There's hardly any glare on paper, you know."

"Whatever makes you happy," chuckled Griffin. "You're carrying your own bags, so I don't care what you bring."

"Fair enough."

Griffin was ultra focused on the extra item that he had packed. He kept checking his pocket so that the little velvet bag was safely tucked away.

Jessica and Griffin had boarded the ship without any issues and soon found their cabin to be adorable. It was bright and roomy feeling, but Jessica was glad to see there were blackout curtains, too. Now they were sitting on their private balcony looking through the ship's schedule of events.

"I mean, I hate crowds, but it seems like a no brainer to head down to the Social Mingle. We might strike up some friendships and there's free food." Jessica hated crowds, but she could push through for a couple of days before she would need to hole up with a book and recharge her social battery.

"Sure. Let's wander around and explore and then end up there. Oh, and check in at our life boat section, so they know we know where it is," Griffin agreed.

"Bring the map, or actually, that's a QR code. Can I bring it up on my phone?" Jessica was pleasantly surprised to see that she could pull up the maps of the ship and then link to the daily activities right on their phones. So much easier!

"Oh, and Mike said we should find a good photo spot for as we leave the dock. Post a leaving picture and ten people will leave us alone."

"Yeah," said Jessica sarcastically, "and then everyone knows we're gone and to break into our house."

"Hmm. Spoilsport." But Griffin saw her point and didn't push it.

"Actually," added Jessica, "I think he said something about there's usually a bunch of wandering shows the first day as people settle in. Music for sure, but also like belly dancing and acrobats by the pool; that sorta thing."

"I wonder if they fall in?" Griffin mused.

"The acrobats? Hopefully not." Jessica giggled, "Unless they're clowns."

They wandered the ship with no particular destination after their required safety check in. Eventually, they ended up having a snack and posing for a caricature artist. Griffin whispered something to the man, but Jessica ignored Griffin, assuming it would be just a suggestion to give her a butterfly perched on her nose or something. The artist smiled and nodded vigorously.

When the man signaled it was done, he motioned for Griffin to look first and wouldn't let Jessica see. She rolled her eyes and laughed, but truthfully was a little irritated. After a moment, Griffin shook the artist's hand and paid him. "It's perfect, thank you."

Griffin motioned her over, and the artist said, "Come see what he asked for. That was such an irritating surprise for you." He spoke with such an outrageous false French accent that Jessica couldn't help but smile. "No, but seriously," the artist continued, "I hope you like it." He held the paper so Jessica could stand beside him and look.

He had done an incredible job capturing their characters, Griffin with a happy golden retriever attitude and herself, shy and happy. But then, looking at more than the faces, Jessica was surprised to see that the image had Griffin down on one knee and holding out a ring.

"Wait, what-?"

The artist moved the paper, and there was Griffin down on one knee in front of Jessica. He had a tiny blue velvet pouch on his hand and nestled on it was a gorgeous silver ring sparling in the light.

Jessica's hand flew to her mouth as her gaze jumped from the ring to Griffin's eyes.

"Will you spend the rest of your life going on cruises with me, Jessica? And the rest of the year working with me to pay for them?"

"What?" Jessica burst out laughing. "That's the most ridiculous proposal I've ever heard!" She paused only a moment. "But yes! Completely yes!"

"Good!" Griffin stood up and kissed her full lips, trying to be sweet and slip on the ring at the same time. But it was harder than it sounded and he broke the kiss to look down at what he was doing. Meanwhile, the crowd had noticed what was going on and began clapping. Jessica flushed scarlet at being the center of attention.

The artist came to her rescue and held up the picture to block her face from some people. "See what can happen from a silly picture?" he called.

A young woman pushed a confused young man up. "I think we're next!" she laughed.

"Ok?" asked Griffin, holding Jessica's gaze."

"Um, yeah," Jessica answered quietly. "You kinda caught me by surprise."

Griffin grinned, "Yeah, that was the idea. C'mon, I'll grab his picture of us and we'll get away from the crowd."

Jessica looked down at the ring. It was perfect. Silver with alternating diamonds and emeralds. Small stones, but she bet they were perfect stones. A perfect balance of color. Everything in her life was coming into balance.

Jessica smiled at Griffin as he took her hand, and they slipped out of the crowd.

The End

Author's note:

I very much hope you enjoyed this story! In which case, a review would mean the world to me - indie authors desperately need reviews for the bigger platforms to even show our books.

If you enjoyed this story, you might also enjoy *Parallel Worlds*[1]. You can find all of my stories here on my Linktree: https://linktr.ee/authorrachelroy. I would love for you to join my reader groups on Facebook and/or join my early access on Ream! Never forget, authors love to hear from you, too, so please reach out by email or social media.

Thank you for your support and have a wonderful day!

Rachel Roy

---

1.   *https://www.amazon.com/Parallel-Worlds-Rachel-Roy-ebook/dp/B0C83MXKMR*

Don't miss out!

Visit the website below and you can sign up to receive emails whenever Rachel Roy publishes a new book. There's no charge and no obligation.

https://books2read.com/r/B-A-EEVR-CNQZE

BOOKS 2 READ

Connecting independent readers to independent writers.

About the Author

Rachel Roy lives in the Northeast Kingdom of Vermont with her husband and children. She has been writing for as long as she has known that people could create books. In 2021, her first children's story, Growing Up As Fairies, first appeared on Kindle Vella in serial format. After edits and illustrations she published it in print in December 2022. In the meantime she added six other series to Kindle Vella including another children's story, two non-fiction homesteading resources, and several fantasy and fantasy romances. Rachel also teaches middle school Humanities as she continues to write.

Read more at https://www.authorrachelroy.com.